WEASEL

Other Avon Camelot Books by
Cynthia DeFelice

DEVIL'S BRIDGE
THE LIGHT ON HOGBACK HILL
LOSTMAN'S RIVER
THE STRANGE NIGHT WRITING OF JESSAMINE COLTER

CYNTHIA DeFELICE, a former school media specialist, is now a professional storyteller, part of the Wild Washerwomen team, which appears at schools, libraries, workshops, and festivals. She and her husband have two children and live in Geneva, New York.

WEASEL

CYNTHIA DeFELICE

AN AVON  CAMELOT BOOK

AVON BOOKS, INC.
195 Broadway,
New York, NY 10007

First Avon Camelot Special Printing: September 1991
First Avon Camelot Printing: October 1991

CAMELOT TRADEMARK REG. U.S. PAT. OFF. AND IN OTHER COUNTRIES, MARCA REGISTRADA,
HECHO EN U.S.A.

Printed in the U.S.A.

18 19 20 BRR 40 39 38 37 36 35 34 33 32 31

1

THE STATE OF
OHIO, 1839 ...

THE dogs were dozing in their usual places by the fire when the knock came.

My sister, Molly, and I jumped. Who could be stopping at our cabin, so deep in the woods, so far from town, so late at night?

Pa! I thought. But, no, Pa wouldn't knock. He'd come right through the door, white teeth smiling through his dark whiskers, brown eyes dancing, and say, "I'm back! Who's got a hug for me?" And I would run and—

Knock knock knock.

Duffy and Winston were fully roused by then and began barking wildly. They jumped at the cabin door, sniffing and whining. Molly and I joined them.

"Who's there?" called Molly.

No one answered. But again—

Knock knock.

I opened the door a few inches and peered into the darkness.

A man stood in the shadows, back a ways from the cabin. I knew it was a man, but he made me think of a wild creature. He was shy of the cabin and the light from the doorway. I had the feeling he might turn and run, like an animal that senses danger.

He was dressed like no white man I had ever seen, in tattered clothing and what looked like animal skins. I could make out a tall hat and long, tangled hair. His beard was dark and so were his eyes, which were looking right into mine.

The dogs stopped barking and stood quietly, staring at the stranger. We stared, too, waiting for him to speak. Finally Molly said, "Who are you? What do you want?"

Without saying a word, the man reached into the leather pouch that hung over his shoulder. He found something and held it out in his hand with his palm open. It gleamed, shiny and golden.

Molly took it and held it up in the lantern light. She gasped.

"Mama's locket!" I cried.

2

MAMA'S locket—Pa had
given it to her the day they were married. It was real
gold and shaped like a heart. Mama had worn it every
day. Inside was a tiny lock of Pa's hair, a bit of Molly's,
and some of mine, too. "So you'll always be with me,
wherever I go," Mama used to say.

On the day Mama died of the fever, Pa cut a lock
of *her* hair and placed it in the locket. He put that
locket on under his shirt and he never took it off, not
even for washing up.

If this man had Mama's locket, he must have seen
Pa. Maybe he knew where Pa was right now. Maybe—

"Where did you get this?" Molly asked, and she sounded scared.

I figured she was thinking the same thing I was: Pa would never take off the locket unless he had a good reason. Or unless someone made him take it off. But who? And why?

"Where's our Pa?" I shouted. My voice seemed strange to me.

Still the man stood silent. Then, slowly, he crooked his finger at us and beckoned.

"He wants us to go with him!" I exclaimed.

"To Papa!" said Molly, but her voice faded to a whisper.

Molly and I looked at each other for a long moment.

Six days before, our pa had gone out hunting. "I'll be back in a few hours with something for supper," he had said. But he hadn't come back. The hours had turned into days, long days filled with listening and looking for Pa.

Being as I was eleven years old, and Molly nine, we knew how to do most everything around the farm. I chopped wood and kept the fire going. Molly made bread and stew. We fed the animals, we fetched the water, we did everything we knew to keep things right. And we waited. That was the worst part. No matter what else we were doing, we were waiting.

"He'll be back tomorrow," I'd say to Molly as we ate our supper.

"He probably got so much meat he can hardly carry it all!" Molly would say.

But we didn't really believe it, and after a few days we ran out of things to say. We didn't dare say what we both were thinking: Something must have happened to Pa.

Then that night, as we were eating our stew, Molly had begun to cry softly.

I had wanted to cry, too, but I couldn't. Pa had said to me, "Take care of things while I'm gone, Nathan. You're the oldest, and you're the man of the house when I'm away."

Pa had smiled as he spoke, but I knew he meant what he said. I kept saying the words over and over to myself: the man of the house. But *Pa* was the man of the house! What would Pa do? It didn't help to think about that; it only got me tangled up and confused, because if Pa was here, everything would be all right.

I turned to the stranger.

"Where do you want to take us?" I asked.

Again, no answer, just the beckoning hand.

Molly looked at me and shrugged. "Why won't he talk to us?" she whispered.

"I don't know," I said. "Maybe . . . he can't. Maybe

he can't even hear us."

"But he must know where Papa is. He has Mama's locket," Molly said.

There was a silence while we both thought about what to do.

"He's so strange, Nathan," Molly said.

I looked again at the man standing in the shadows. He *was* strange ... but I had a feeling about him. Maybe he had hurt Pa and taken the locket. But I didn't think so.

An idea came upon me all of a sudden. Maybe Pa sent the locket as a sign to us.

"Molly, I think we should go with him," I said. "It's the only way we'll find out what happened to Pa. We know he'd have come home if he could. What if he needs our help? He could have sent the locket so we'd know to come. And, well, seems like anything's better than waiting here, not knowing."

I thought about how she had clung to the dogs the last few days for comfort. "We can take Duffy and Win with us," I added.

Molly looked at the stranger again, then looked at me and nodded. "You're right, Nathan, anything's better than just sitting here, waiting. Let's go. I'll get us some warm clothes," she said, and turned back inside.

I called into the shadows, "Please wait. We need

to get some supplies." There was no answer.

Inside I gathered food and put it in my pack. Molly added warm clothing, then said, "I'll bring this, too." She was holding Mama's medicine bag. Slowly I nodded, but I didn't like to think that we would need it.

I put out the fire and took the kettle off the hook where it hung. I poured a cup of the strong herb tea Molly had made, the kind Pa liked, and took it out to the stranger. The man held the cup awkwardly with two hands and gulped. When he handed it back, he reached up and touched me, just for a moment, on the shoulder. Then he turned and started into the woods.

"Molly!" I called. Molly, Duffy, and Win came running out of the darkened cabin, and off we went to find Pa—we hoped.

3

THE man slipped through the forest like a shadow. At first he moved so quickly and quietly that I was sure we would be left behind. Then he slowed his pace to match ours as we stumbled through the darkness, tripping over roots, our clothing catching in the branches. Duffy and Win moved along easily, and after a while, when Molly and I got used to the darkness, we moved faster, too. Once I fell, and a strong arm caught and held me until I got my balance. Later I heard Molly stumble and cry out, then whisper, "Thank you."

In the beginning I tried to keep track of where we were going, but soon I gave it up. The twisted paths weren't familiar to me, and it took almost all of my concentration just to stay on my feet and keep up. I kept an eye on the bright star in the north and reckoned we were traveling due west.

My thoughts were racing around and around in my head, but going nowhere. Like when Duffy and Win chase their tails, I thought. One minute I'd think about seeing Pa again, and I'd feel real good. Then I'd think: You're acting like a darn fool, heading out in the middle of the night to follow a complete stranger, and I'd start to feel scared. The man has Mama's locket, I argued with myself. That means Pa sent him for us ... doesn't it? "Yes!" I wasn't sure if I had cried aloud or not.

We kept on. I felt near worn out from the worrying and the walking. Molly began to fall behind, and I held on to her arm and tried to think of something that would make her feel hopeful. "I reckon we're getting close to Pa now!" I said.

Molly nodded and smiled, but said nothing.

We came to a narrow ledge, and I had to let go of Molly's arm to walk single file. On our left rose the sheer wall of a steep mountain cliff. The land dropped off real sharp to the right and below us flowed the big river, the one the Shawnee Indians called the "Big Turkey" River and we called the Ohio.

The sun was coming up, and its tender light was

shining through the trees and touching the rock cliff where we stood. The river looked like it was on fire, all pink and orange and bright. Mama always said things seem better in the morning. I could feel my spirits rising with the sun.

In the dawn light I saw Molly's face, pale with tiredness. Looking ahead for our leader, I saw that the stranger, too, had stopped and was watching the world turn from night to day. Something about the way he stood kept me from speaking. It's almost as if he's praying, I thought.

Then the man turned to us and slowly nodded. It seemed like a greeting and then some, like he was saying something about the sun coming up and how good it was. I nodded in return.

"Good morning, sir," I said. The night had passed in almost complete silence, and it felt queer to be speaking now. I continued uncertainly, "Please, could we stop for a spell? We brought a bit of food. We'd be proud if you'd share it with us."

I waited, not knowing if the man would answer or even hear.

"It would feel good to rest, sir," said Molly. She added shyly, "You must be tired, too."

The stranger pointed ahead to a wider spot on the trail. Molly and I looked at each other with relief. We followed and watched our companion sit down among the rocks and leaves. As soon as he was still, he seemed to blend in with his surroundings. Awkwardly we sat down, too, and the dogs settled in close as Molly broke the bread and I cut pieces from the chunk of venison I had put in the pack.

The man took the food we offered with another sober nod. The pale morning light gave us our first good look at him. I knew it wasn't polite to stare at folks, but still, I couldn't take my eyes off him. I'd seen a few Shawnees, the Indians who used to live in these parts before they were all driven off. This man looked like one of them, except he was a white man, not an Indian. He wore cloth trousers like Pa's, but his shirt, leggings, and moccasins were fashioned of buckskin, and so was the pouch that hung around his neck. The moccasins were all prettied up with beadwork and some things that looked like they might be the stickers off a porcupine's back. Everything he wore appeared to be held together with strips of hide, some rawhide and some with the fur left on. Around his neck were necklaces, one of rawhide strung with the teeth and claws of animals, and one of threaded blue glass beads.

His hair was long, and held on either side of his head with strips of cloth. He wore a tall black hat like I had seen in a picture of Andrew Jackson when he was the president. It was pulled down low over his ears and eyes. With the hat and the way he sat so straight and looked so serious, he was pretty near as dignified as Mr. Jackson himself.

I pointed to the man's hat and said, "It's a very nice hat, sir. I'd like to have a hat like that someday."

To my astonishment, the man's mouth suddenly turned up in a huge grin. His eyes got all crinkled up, and his eyebrows and even his ears wiggled. It was something to see. Molly and I were right taken aback at first, but soon we were grinning, too. Then, real abrupt, his face changed. It turned so cold and fearsome it took my breath away.

His eyes got all squinty, looking right past us like we weren't even there in front of him. I tried to follow his eyes, over to the other side of the river. At first all I saw was the forest and the river flowing by nice and peaceful. Then I noticed a flicker of movement and focused on a man slipping quick and sly through a stand of birch trees. I caught just a glimpse of a lean body, a large head with a strong, thick neck, and brown hair with what looked like a patch of white up front. Even as I watched, the figure vanished in the thin dawn light, till I wasn't sure I had even seen it.

I turned back to our companion and was relieved to see the murderous look gone from his face. What's he doing now? I wondered. Using his hands, he was clearing away the leaves that lay on the path. Then he found a stick, smoothed the dirt, and wrote:

WEEZL

Molly and I read the word aloud together. Weasel!

"That was Weasel?" I asked. My heart started thumping in my chest.

The man nodded.

"He *is* real, then," said Molly, and the words seemed to stick in her throat.

4

WEASEL! The name had haunted my sleep and made my wide-awake hours uneasy for as long as I could remember. Once, when Molly and I were just four and six years old, Mama and Pa took us to town. They bought supplies and talked to the grown-ups while Molly and I played with the other children. The children whispered to us strange tales about Weasel. They said he was part man and part animal and called him wild and blood-thirsty. They said he preyed on settlers like us. He came in the dark of night, killing whole families and stealing whatever they had.

That night, terrified, we asked Mama and Pa about

the creature called Weasel. Pa said, "It's pure non-sense, nothing to worry about. You know how folks like to talk."

And Pa made us laugh trying to imagine a creature who was part man and part animal, and Mama rocked us and sang.

But later, when I woke with a bad dream, I heard Mama and Pa talking. I learned that Weasel was real, but he wasn't really part animal. He was a man, an Indian fighter. The government had sent him out to make the state of Ohio safe for settlers. His job was to drive the Indians off—"remove them," Pa said—to Kansas. Pa said Weasel had his own ideas about removal, and most often it meant killing.

Pa said, "He did his job, all right. The Shawnee named him 'Weasel' in their language because he hunted them down just like a weasel. He's cunning. He's not a big man, but he's fearless. Like a weasel, he hunts by night and sleeps by day, and he kills not because he's hungry, but for the sheer sport of it. They say he even looks like a weasel. He's tall and slender, and his hair is brown with a big shock of white in the front. It's that hair that reminds folks so much of the animal. You know how when a weasel is halfway into its molt, it shows part of its white winter coat and part of its brown summer coat? That's the way he looks, I guess. And just like a weasel, they say he can pass through any opening big enough for his head to get through."

"Remember when that weasel got into the henhouse?" said Mama. "It killed every single bird. It didn't eat them or take them home to feed its young. It just . . . killed them." Mama's voice was shaky, remembering.

Then I heard Pa say, "And now that the Shawnees are dead or driven off, they say that Weasel has turned on us settlers. Shoot, folks fear him more than they ever feared the Shawnees."

"But why?" Mama asked. "Why is he killing the very people he was sent to protect?"

"I reckon when a man's been killing his whole life, something happens inside him, and he can't see any other way," Pa said.

"But what about us?" asked Mama. "What about the children? Are we safe?"

"Duffy and Win aren't about to let any Weasel sneak up on us," said Pa. "And you know how to shoot that rifle as well as I do, pretty near. I guess it wouldn't hurt to start teaching Nathan, though," he added.

I didn't tell Molly about what I heard that night, but the next day I asked Pa to teach me to shoot. I practiced and practiced until Pa joked, "Why, son, you're almost as good a shot as your ma!"

MOLLY and I looked up, round eyed, at the stranger, both of us asking questions at the same time.

"Are those horrible stories about him true?"

"Is he as cruel as they say?"

The man looked at us steadily for a long time, as if he was trying to decide how to answer our questions. I was sure he was going to speak to us at last. Instead, he opened his mouth wide and leaned forward. We stared into a gaping, black hole. At first I couldn't make sense of what I was seeing. And then I realized that where his tongue should have been, there was nothing, nothing at all.

5

I FROZE. I couldn't move or speak. Molly gave a low moan and began to cry noiselessly. The tears streamed down her face as she stared at the stranger, her eyes wide with shock.

The man leaned forward again, this time to touch us each gently. I felt like he was willing us to look at him. Do not be afraid, his eyes said. Do not pity me.

"Sir," I whispered, "did Weasel do that to you?"

He nodded.

I swallowed hard, then asked, "What is your name?"

Again the man took the stick and scratched in the earth:

EZRA

"Ezra, sir," I said, "my name is Nathan Fowler, and this is my sister, Molly, and we're . . . we're pleased to know you, sir."

Ezra nodded and smiled faintly. I went on. "I wonder if you might tell us, are you taking us to our father?"

A nod.

"Where is he?" burst out Molly. "Is he all right?"

Ezra stood up and motioned for us to follow him once again. Quickly we packed up the food and started after him down the trail. I felt numb from the long night of walking and the horrible truth about Ezra's silence.

Molly and I walked without speaking, lost in our own thoughts. Another hour passed, and the sun rose higher and the air began to warm.

At a point where the path ran close to the river, Ezra suddenly stepped off into the underbrush, glancing behind to make sure we were following. We walked several hundred yards through some sticker bushes, then into a stand of mixed pine and maple trees.

At first I didn't see the little dwelling, it blended in so well with its surroundings. It was what the Shawnees called a *we-gi-wa*, a shelter made of poles and bark. Some poles had been planted upright in the ground. More poles had been laid crossways on top of those and tied in place with thongs of hickory bark. Then sheets of elm bark had been added to make sides and a roof.

Ezra pulled aside a large flap of bark that covered the doorway. Molly and I stepped inside. I was shaking, wondering what we would find. I grabbed Molly's hand and held on.

A small amount of light came through a smoke hole in the center of the roof. We paused for a moment, to give our eyes time to adjust to the semi-darkness.

Under the smoke hole was a circle of stones for the fire, surrounded by a few utensils: a copper pot, a larger brass kettle, some wooden bowls, tin cups, and pewter and horn spoons. At the far end of the room was a platform made of buckskins stretched over wooden poles. There were a few blankets on the platform. Under them lay a quiet figure.

"Papa!" Molly and I cried together. We rushed across the room. Duffy and Win ran past us and began joyously licking Pa's face, their tails thumping furiously. We stared down at our father. He seemed to have shrunk since I last saw him. He lay absolutely still, eyes closed, taking only shallow, irregular breaths. His face was deathly pale, except for a bright pink spot on each cheek.

Molly threw her arms around him and kissed his face. She drew back with alarm.

"He's burning up with fever, Nathan! Just like . . . just like Mama! Oh, Papa, Papa, please don't die!"

Molly turned to me and sobbed. I held her, near tears myself, and watched as Ezra walked over to Pa and gently pulled back the blankets.

Pa's left trouser leg was cut off, revealing a wound that circled around his calf. The skin and flesh were badly shredded, and they had been sewed back together with neat, little stitches. But I knew that the swelling and the pale yellowish green oozing were bad signs. Pa was sick, all right, but he didn't have the fever, like Mama had had.

I stroked Molly's hair and said, "Molly, Pa's not going to die." I hoped I was telling the truth. "His fever is from the wound. It looks like he stepped in a trap. . . ."

I looked at Ezra, who hesitated, then nodded.

"Remember when Mama sewed up Gideon Thurstan's leg after he cut it open with his axe? Look, Ezra has sewn up Pa's leg the same way. If we can heal the festering around the wound, Pa will be well again. Molly, do you remember what Mama did for flesh that looked like this?"

Molly brought over the soft pouch made of tanned leather—Mama's medicine bag. Carefully, she untied the thongs and opened it, and we saw lots of small pockets filled with the stems, leaves, flowers, and roots of plants. Some were common, as familiar to me as the big oak tree that grew outside our cabin. Others were rare and much more difficult to find. Some, the ones Mama used to call her treasures, were from faraway places like China and Mexico. She told us these herbs had traveled many miles, been traded back and forth, and passed through many hands before they had reached her bag.

When the bag was opened, Mama came back in a rush of exotic smells. I could almost see her walking slowly through the forest, exclaiming when she found a particular plant, holding it up for us to see, showing us how to recognize it by sight and smell. I remembered Mama, humming to herself, sorting and arranging the herbs in her bag. She would pound the roots of some, dry the leaves or crumble the flowers of others, preparing them to make what she called infusions, or poultices, or soothing ointments.

It was Molly, not me, who Mama had really tried to teach about healing. She said menfolk were always going off and getting themselves hurt, and someone had to know how to care for them. But it was Mama who had gotten the fever and died, and none of the medicine in the world had been able to help her.

Molly looked at the contents of the bag, and a panicked look came over her face. "Nathan, I can't remember what to do," she wailed. "Papa's going to die because of me, because I didn't listen carefully to Mama's lessons. I—I thought there was lots of time to learn. . . ."

Ezra came over to Molly. He placed one hand on her shoulder, and with the other he took the medicine bag from her hand. He handed her Mama's locket and nodded his head toward Pa. Grateful to have something to do, she went to Pa's bed and gently placed the locket around his neck.

"There," I heard her whisper, "that's better, isn't it, Papa?"

Maybe it was silly, but somehow I felt having the locket back would help Pa get well.

Ezra was reaching into the bag, passing by some of the pockets, pulling the contents out of others to see, sniff, and feel. Finally he held up a whitish root and some dried green leaves.

Then Molly said, "I remember Mama boiling those leaves—witch hazel, they're called—in water. She used it to bathe Mr. Thurstan's wound. I'll do the

24

same thing for Papa, Ezra," she added shyly.

She set a pot on to boil as Ezra took the root and ground it to a fine, white powder. He added water and a small amount of bear oil. While Molly and I watched closely, he took a cloth and washed Pa's wound with the solution that Molly had made. It smelled clean and strong. Then Ezra applied a poultice made from the white root. He searched the bag again until he found some more leaves. Molly said Mama had used them to make Mr. Thurstan tea.

"I'll make some now," said Molly.

Now that she saw that Ezra knew about healing, the frightened look on her face disappeared, and she began to remember some of the things Mama had told her.

"I'll add some elm bark to give Papa strength. And tonight we'll make tea from these and these," she said, pointing proudly to some dried flowers. "They'll help Papa to sleep soundly."

Ezra nodded and smiled at us. I smiled back. It felt good after all the days of worry and fear.

Ezra handed me a basket of dried corn. He showed me how to grind the corn so that the kernel separated from the skin. Then he put the broken kernels into a broad, shallow basket, and to our surprise, he took the basket outside and began waving it about in the air!

It was a strange sight, the tall, thin, oddly clad man twirling about in the clearing. Bits of fur and feathers danced and flapped, and small particles came flying out of the basket as it swirled around and around. We began to laugh out loud. Ezra looked over at us and smiled. When the dance was over, he showed us what was left in the basket. The skins and chaff had blown away, and only the kernels of corn remained. We watched as Ezra made a very fine powder from the kernels, added water, and put the mixture over the fire to boil.

Molly and I took turns slowly spooning the soft, watery cornmeal mush into Pa's mouth and giving him sips of the strong, healing tea as the day turned slowly to night.

I wasn't afraid of Ezra, but I sure wondered about him. He was a white man, but his house was an Indian house, his ways were Indian ways. I could see he was accustomed to living alone, but there was plenty of room in the we-gi-wa for all four of us. Even here, in his own home, he still made me think of a wild creature. He was so wary and alert. And though his eyes were kind when he smiled, it seemed that most of the time they stared off into a place that only Ezra could see. Wherever it is, it's not a very happy place, I thought.

Something else was bothering me. Pa never went

anywhere without his gun. He had taken it with him the day he disappeared. But it was nowhere to be seen in Ezra's dwelling. I noticed a bow and some arrows by the door, and a piece of wood I figured to be some kind of weapon, but no gun.

Although I was very tired, I slept fitfully, and I could feel Molly restless beside me. I awoke once to the soft glow of the banked fire, the shadows flickering on the bark walls and roof, and the sounds of the wind outside the we-gi-wa, and wondered, Where am I?

Pa's shallow breathing brought back the day before in a rush. Molly moaned in her sleep. Duffy and Win pricked up their ears, then settled back to sleep.

I woke several times more, drenched with sweat and breathing hard. Once I dreamed that Mama was trying to explain to me the secrets of the medicine bag, to tell me about a special mixture that would make Pa well. But Mama was far away, so far, and no matter how hard I tried, I couldn't quite hear what she was saying. . . .

Then I dreamed of Weasel. Weasel was outside the we-gi-wa. He was creeping, weasellike, around the lodge, looking for an opening. Around his neck hung a rawhide strip. Something dangled from it, and I realized with horror that it was Ezra's tongue. In Weasel's hand was Pa's gun. . . .

6

MORNING came at last. When I opened my eyes, Ezra, the bow and arrows, and the dogs were nowhere to be seen. Molly was sitting with Pa, talking softly to him, spooning sips of tea and small bites of cornmeal mush into his mouth.

"I think Papa seems better today, Nathan. Come see!" she called. It did seem that Pa's face was a more normal color, and the hectic red spots on his cheeks were gone. But his skin felt hot, and it frightened me to see him so still and quiet—and helpless.

"He needs more medicine," I said.

"The white root is gone," Molly said, "and there aren't many tea fixings left. But Ezra seems to know

28

about healing," she added hopefully. Then she whispered, "Nathan, don't you wish he could talk to us? There's so much I want to ask him, but it doesn't feel right to talk to him when he can't answer." She shuddered, remembering. "I can't bear to think about it."

"I know, Molly. I wish he could tell us what happened, how Pa got here. I keep thinking, how did Ezra know about us? He saved Pa's life, it looks like, and then came to get us, to bring us here. I thought the locket meant Pa sent him for us, but Pa's too sick for that. Ezra just came."

As if he had heard my words, Ezra appeared, followed by Duffy and Winston. He set down the bow and arrows by the door and held something high up over his head. The dogs jumped up on him and danced on their hind legs trying to reach it, and we saw that it was a wild turkey. We were startled to hear Ezra suddenly laugh aloud, the first sound we had heard him make. As the turkey flapped its wings feebly, and the dogs lunged and licked, we laughed, too.

"Down, Duff! Down, Win!" I said in my deepest voice, trying to sound like Pa. To my surprise, the dogs gave one last leap toward the turkey and lay down in their places by the fire, gazing longingly at Ezra.

Molly and I watched Ezra clean the bird. He didn't

waste anything. The feathers he placed carefully in a skin bag. He put the meat, along with the bones, in the kettle and added berries and squash. Molly's eyes grew large, and she made a face at me as Ezra took ashes from a bowl and mixed them with some of the cornmeal mush. He added water and a small amount of maple syrup to make a bluish-colored dough, which he shaped into three-cornered biscuits and dropped into the boiling pot. Our mouths watered at the smell of the cooking food. We had had no fresh meat since Pa left.

While the pot simmered, Ezra removed the poultice from Pa's leg, and Molly bathed the wound again. I watched Ezra's face as he looked at Pa's leg, but I couldn't read anything in it.

7

SUDDENLY, with a feeling of shame, I remembered the animals. In the rush to follow Ezra and find Pa, I had forgotten all about them. I'd left them without food or water for—how long had it been? Two mornings? Yes, this was the second morning. I had broken Pa's first rule: Before I did anything else each day, I had to care for the animals.

I remembered him explaining: "If a man's going to keep animals to work for him and feed him, he's got an obligation to treat them right. A man who mistreats a poor, dumb beast is no better than a beast himself."

I could never face Pa if I left those animals to die of hunger and thirst. I jumped up and started putting on my boots. Ezra and Molly turned to stare at me.

"I have to go," I said. "Back home. To feed the animals."

In the quiet of the little room, my outburst seemed very loud. "I have to feed them. They depend on me."

Ezra looked worried, and Molly began, "Nathan, you can't go—"

"I have to go. And I have an idea," I said. "I can bring Job and Crabapple—that's our horse and our mule," I added for Ezra's sake, "back with me. I'll ride Job and lead Crabby. I'll get back quicker, and that way Pa will have a way to get back home if his leg doesn't—if he—if it doesn't heal right," I finished quietly.

Molly stared at me. Her eyes looked huge. I could tell Ezra was trying to decide what to do.

"If you draw me a map, I can find my way," I said. "In the daylight it won't take so long, and on horseback I'll be back before dark tonight."

Still Ezra hesitated.

I understood. "You don't want me to go by myself, do you?"

Ezra shook his head.

"But we can't leave Pa alone again. The medicine is helping him, but Molly says it's almost gone. If you and Molly can find more of the white root and the right kind of leaves and watch over Pa, I'll be back by nightfall and everything will be fine. I can't think of any other way, Ezra. I can't leave those animals to die."

Ezra nodded, and I followed him outside. In the soft dirt under a pine tree, he drew a picture. Pointing to the sky, he drew a star.

"The star off the tip of the Dipper?" I asked. "The one that points north?"

He nodded. Next he gestured all around us and drew an X on the map. The X was Ezra's house. Then he drew the sun in the sky, with an arrow showing the path the sun would take as the day passed. He added the big river, the sheer cliffs we had passed, the softer, rolling hills, and finally the valley where our cabin stood surrounded by the forest. Carefully he added the small streams that came into the big river, then other things that would help me find my way, like large boulders, groves of trees, and swampy areas.

When he was satisfied with the drawing, he drew a path through it for me to follow. I knew there was not really a path, but that this would be the easiest way to travel. I looked carefully as Ezra emphasized by pointing, shaking or nodding his head, frowning or smiling, which twists and turns to take and which to avoid. I studied the picture for a long time, memorizing every detail.

Molly brought me a bowl of the turkey stew with some of the bluish biscuits floating in it. I was real hungry, but the sight of those blue biscuits stopped me. Then I noticed Ezra watching me anxiously, so I took a taste. It was good. I ate it all and got myself some more, and Ezra seemed pleased. Molly rolled up more biscuits in some wild grape leaves and put them in my pockets.

"Be careful, Nathan," she said, and I could tell she was trying hard not to cry.

I whispered, "You're not afraid to stay with Ezra, are you?"

She shook her head and said bravely, "When you come back tonight, Papa will be much better, you'll see!"

She reached up to kiss and hug me hard, something she had not done for a long time.

"I'll be back before you know it, Molly," I said, hugging her back. "And I'll tell Miz Tizz and her piglets you say howdy."

That made Molly laugh. Ezra, it seemed, had one last thing he wanted to show me. He got the odd, club-shaped piece of wood I had noticed next to the door. Taking me back outside, he pointed into the forest, then got down on all fours and imitated a running animal. Next he stood up and continued pretending to run, on two legs now. Then, himself again, he pointed once more into the forest, picked up the piece of wood, and with a peculiar twist of his arm, threw it in the direction he had pointed. It twirled, spinning over and over itself, until it landed on the ground where Ezra had pointed. Then, while he pretended to be running again, Ezra's legs suddenly buckled under him, and he fell to the ground.

He stood up somewhat sheepishly and looked at me. He lifted up his eyebrows as if to say, Do you see? I nodded. The piece of wood was a weapon, just like I thought. It was probably used by the Shawnees. I thought that whatever—or whoever—Ezra threw it at would get tripped up and fall down for sure. But I didn't think the same thing would happen if I threw it.

I ran to get the stick. "I want to learn how to do that!" I said. "But I don't have time to practice with it now. What happened to Pa's gun? I know how to use that."

For the second time, Ezra's face was transformed by hatred. This time I knew what that look meant.

"Weasel?" I asked. I couldn't believe it. My dream came back to me vividly. "Weasel has Pa's gun?" I repeated stupidly.

Ezra nodded.

"Ezra, what happened? What does Weasel have to do with Pa? How did he get the gun?"

We stared at each other. I wanted him to speak so bad, I almost felt like if I looked at him long enough, he would. Someday, I thought, I'll find out the whole story. But if I didn't leave right away, I'd never get back before nightfall.

I put the club in my pack, more to ease Ezra's mind than anything else. Molly called a last good-bye. I took Ezra's hand awkwardly and shook it. Then I turned and began the longest journey of my life.

8

KEEPING Ezra's picture
in my mind, I retraced the steps I had made so hes-
itatingly in the dark two nights before. The air held
the chill of October, but the sun was shining, warming
my face and making the autumn colors of the trees
glow. As I walked, I thought of other autumn days,
when Mama was still alive, before Pa was hurt. On
days like today, I'd be out helping Pa in the field,
bringing in our harvest of squash, corn, and beans,
or practicing with my slingshot, or playing catch with
Molly, trying to keep the ball away from Duffy and
Winston. Tears sprang suddenly to my eyes, and I

brushed them angrily away. Those days are gone, I told myself, and they'll never come back.

I headed east, keeping the sun to my right, looking for the landmarks Ezra had drawn. In the late afternoon, I began to recognize places in the forest where I had been hunting with Pa. Soon I was standing on a ridge, looking down at the opening in the trees that we had worked so hard to clear. I saw our cabin and our fields. They weren't green anymore, but had on their harvest colors of brown and orange and yellow. I could see the animal pens and Mama's small flower garden that Molly and I had tried to keep up. It was strange, looking at our farm that way. I had always thought of it as being so big and safe and proud. But looking down at it now, it looked like it was made from the little carved wooden toys Pa and Mama had bought for me from Isaac the Peddler's sack. The woods all around, which usually felt friendly and familiar, seemed cold and uncaring.

Shaking off the feeling, I began to hurry over the last miles to our cabin, thinking about what needed to be done. After feeding and watering all the animals, I'd saddle up Job and load Crabby with hay and grain, enough for a couple of days. I'd fill up the pig's trough with plenty of feed, and scatter lots of corn for the chickens. If I filled the big tub with water, it would last for two or three days. Then, I figured, depending on how long it took for Pa to mend, we'd all come back together, or I'd come myself and tend to the animals again. I was worried that Miz Tizz would eat up all the food the first day and get sick, or that she or the piglets might knock over the water tub, but I guessed it was a chance I'd have to take.

Anxious now to see the animals, I began to run. I thought how glad Job would be to see me. He'd whinny and come over to nuzzle my neck. Crabapple would pretend he didn't much care, but his ears would perk up, anyhow, and give him away. The chickens would do their usual foolish fussing, and Miz Tizz would grunt to let me know that she expected me to scratch her back and behind her ears with a stick.

Stepping into the clearing, I called, "Here, Job! Here, Crabby! Hey, you two! I'm home!" I watched for them to come to the fence, looking for me. But there was no movement, no answering whinny, nothing at all.

I ran through the gate. There was no sign of Job or Crabby in the yard or in the barn. Maybe they got so hungry and thirsty they broke out and wandered off, I thought. I walked along the fence, looking for a break, but the fence was solid. I ran to the shed where we kept the chickens and the pigs.

Something was very wrong, I knew then. It was much too quiet. Even when Job and Crabby were out working, the yard was noisy, filled with clucks and squabbles, grunts and squeals. But an unearthly quiet hung over the yard and made me want to turn and run.

I peered into the shed. In the dim light that filtered through the cracks, I saw the outline of Miss Tizz, lying in her usual corner near the trough. She was so still. There was no snuffle of greeting, no scramble of piglets by her side. I knelt beside her in the semi-darkness and reached out to stroke her head. I quickly drew back my hand. Miz Tizz was cold. Then I saw the blackened hole through her forehead where a bullet had passed. There was no sign of the piglets. Dimly I realized that the dead bodies of chickens lay strewn about the ground.

The sight of the slaughtered animals brought back that night years ago when I lay in my bed, feeling sick and scared, listening to my parents talking about a man called Weasel.

I sat beside Miz Tizz, and I knew that Weasel had been here. He had done this, I was certain. For a moment, I wanted Mama to be there to rock me and sing to me. I wanted Pa to hold me in his strong arms and make me laugh. I wanted to go back to the time before I knew that men could do things like this. You can't go back, I thought, and I felt my face twisting with hatred until I knew I looked the way Ezra looked when he thought of Weasel.

My hatred made me feel strong. I stood up and thought about what to do. I got the shovel from its place in the corner. We had a small cemetery on the north side of the farm. Mama was buried there. Our first horse, Gabriel, was there, and so was a dog, Lallygag, and some other small animals Molly and I had kept as pets.

I would bury Miz Tizz. Pa said once that the difference between savages and civilized men was that civilized men buried their dead.

I pushed her large body onto a feed sack, tied a rope around the whole thing, and dragged it to the cemetery. As I began digging the grave, I remembered asking Pa, "Why do folks call the Shawnees savages, then?" We had seen plenty of Indian burial mounds in the areas where the Indians had been driven off. "They bury their dead same as us."

Pa's answer had been long and complicated and had seemed to make him sad. I didn't really understand all of it. He said white men called the Indians savages because that made it easier to hate them, and hating them made it easier to drive them off or kill them

41

and take their land. He said that as long as folks thought of the Shawnees as savages, they didn't have to think of them as people.

Like I said, I didn't really understand most of it. Of course the Shawnees were people. Just calling a thing something else didn't change it.

I thought about Weasel's cutting out Ezra's tongue and killing Indians and poor settlers and Miz Tizz, too. Seemed to me he was more a savage than anybody I'd ever heard of. Couldn't white folks be savages, too?

I kept digging. In some way I couldn't quite put words to, burying Miz Tizz helped make up for the awful way she had died. It was the only thing I could do for her.

I placed Miz Tizz in the ground, surrounded her with the slaughtered chickens, and filled in the hole. Then I said a few words about how she was the mother of many litters of piglets, and a good mother, too, but then it got hard to talk for crying, so I just finished the rest in my head. Then I turned to go.

Our cabin looked cheerless, dark, and lonely. Even though night was closing in fast, I knew I would start back to Ezra's. I didn't want to spend a night alone here, not when Weasel had been here and could come back. Better, I thought, to be moving through the darkness, back to Molly and Pa and Ezra, than to be here alone. Besides, they were waiting for me. I'd be much later than they expected, and I knew the feeling of waiting for someone to come back.

I guessed that Weasel had ridden off on Job, leading Crabby, like I'd planned to do. He'd probably taken the piglets and a few of the chickens. Miz Tizz, I thought sickly, had been too big to carry, but that hadn't saved her from Weasel.

9

THE shadows were getting longer, making deep pockets of darkness. I closed my eyes to picture Ezra's map and tried to calm myself. I wouldn't have the sun to guide me, and many of the landmarks would be hidden by darkness. The moon, I recalled, was showing about half of itself then, but it wouldn't be rising until later. I had to rely on my memory of a journey taken once in the dark and once in daylight. I'd have to keep my wits about me, as Pa always said. I couldn't let fear get the best of my good sense. Pa said that when a man let his mind get full of something strong like fear or anger, he couldn't think straight. Think of Pa, I told myself. Think of

Molly and Ezra and Duffy and Win, and how they're waiting for you. Think of Mama, and how she's watching over you and keeping you safe. Think of anything except the darkness and Weasel.

I took advantage of the last bit of daylight to run fast and cover as much ground as I could, but finally I had to slow down, as it became very dark. A few stars shone down through the clear, cold air, and a breeze began to sweep through the trees, rustling the leaves and swaying the branches.

The night was coming alive. I heard the cry of the nighthawk and later the *hoo hoohoo hoo hoo* of the great horned owl. As I passed through a stand of hickory trees, I disturbed a group of turkeys who were roosting in the upper branches. They sounded huge as they flew off, crashing through the trees and landing on the ground. When I moved on, I could hear them calling to one another so they could gather again for the night.

Every once in a while, I heard the steps of larger animals moving away from me in the forest. I didn't really belong in their nighttime world. If I concentrated hard, with all my senses alert, I was able to move pretty quickly through the night forest. I may not be very quiet, but I reckon I'm going as fast as Ezra could, I thought proudly.

After a while, the moon came up, and its light made

the going even faster. I was feeling confident and strong. I could even forget the hunger gnawing at my stomach and the urge to look back over my shoulder. Ahead, their steep sides gleaming silver in the moonlight, were the cliffs that rose high above the big river, where we had stopped to rest and eat with Ezra. I felt a smile of satisfaction creep over my face: I had found my way. Only a little over an hour and I'd be at Ezra's. I'd sit by the warm fire, eat some stew. Pa would be awake; he'd lie in his bed and listen while I told about my journey. He'd be proud. I'd see the same pride in Ezra's eyes, and Molly's.

Suddenly my thoughts were interrupted by the sharp snap of a twig behind me. I stopped. I'd become accustomed to the noises of the night and its creatures, and this was new and different. There was something strange, something stealthy about the sudden utter silence. I waited and, hearing nothing else, began to walk again, then stopped quickly and listened.

There was the rustle of footsteps in the leaves, then silence. Whatever was behind me was behaving the way Pa and I did when we were stalking game. I was being stalked like an animal. My heart began to beat in a fast, skittery way, and I could feel prickles down the back of my neck. I realized that I was now near the very place where we were sitting when Ezra spotted Weasel. Slowly and quietly, I slipped behind a rock that jutted out from the cliff. With one hand, I reached behind into my pack until I felt the thick, rounded end of the hunting stick Ezra had given me. Slowly, slowly, I drew it out of the pack, sliding it through my hand until I held the narrower end, as Ezra had done. I waited.

The silence stretched on. It lasted so long I was beginning to distrust my memory. Had I really heard what I thought I heard, or was it my imagination? I had about decided I must have been mistaken and was fixing to step out onto the path again, when a voice broke the stillness and sent a chill racing down my spine.

"You gonna hide there all night, boy?"

I stood frozen. I was so afraid I thought maybe fear was something I could die of, right then and there.

"What's this? Some yellow-bellied Shawnee trick you learned from that white Injun?" There was a hoot of laughter. Then the voice took on a different tone, sounding friendly, but not so I believed it. "You come on out here now and show yourself, boy."

I shifted slightly so I could see between the cliff wall and the large rock that stood between me and the voice. In the path stood a dim figure. Moonlight shone brightly on a shock of white hair and on the barrel of a rifle, making them stand out brilliantly in the darkness.

Weasel. With Pa's gun. Just like in my dream. My dream hadn't told me what happened next, so I just stayed still.

The voice became harsh again, and angry.

"You come on out here now, boy. I ain't got time to play games. I've seen every Injun trick there is, and I'm still standin' right here, now, ain't I? So just show yourself, and maybe you won't have to get hurt."

I didn't answer. It seemed to me I was safe as long as I stayed where I was. How long can we stand here like this? I wondered.

As if I had spoken out loud, Weasel growled, "I'm tired of playin' with ya, boy." He began walking slowly toward my hiding place, the rifle pointed right at me.

I'd been holding Ezra's hunting stick so tight, my fingers felt numb. I drew the stick back in the throwing position and wiggled my fingers to make sure they still worked.

Weasel was about twenty yards away. I didn't know how far I could throw the stick, but I knew I didn't want him to get any closer. I drew a deep breath and jumped out into the narrow path. Focusing on the gleaming rifle, I threw the stick. The last thing I remember was hearing a rifle shot and a long, loud scream, and wondering if it was my voice or Weasel's.

10

WHEN I opened my eyes,
I was half sitting, half lying on a dirt floor in the
corner of a crude cabin. I slowly came to my senses
and tried to move. I couldn't, not much. It took me
a while to figure out I was tied up, with my hands
behind my back and my ankles bound.

I slowly inched my head up so I could see around
the room. My first thought was that Mama wouldn't
think much of this cabin at all. I could see right out
through the chinks between the logs, and a cold draft
blew in at me. It appeared to be still dark out. By the
light from the fire, I saw things were thrown every
which way around the room: dirty blankets and clothes,

unwashed pots and bowls, some animal hides, which, not being properly tanned, stunk something awful.

I could hear considerable cussing and muttering from the opposite corner. I wriggled slightly so I could look in that direction. Weasel sat on the floor, a large knife in his hand. He was digging at his ankle with the knife and saying words I'd never heard the likes of before. He appeared not to have noticed that I was awake, and I closed one eye so as to be ready to look like I was still asleep if he glanced my way.

His face was red and kind of wild looking. From time to time, he'd let off cussing to take a big swallow from a jug that sat next to him on the floor. Then he'd clench his teeth so the muscles in his jaw bulged out and commence digging at his ankle again.

I caught little bits of what he was muttering in between all the cuss words. It seemed he was right put out about the fact that in "twenty years of fightin' Injuns," he hadn't got shot once, but here "some squirt of a boy" had made him shoot himself in his own leg. As I listened, it came to me that the boy was me. I felt right proud, though I wasn't real clear on what exactly had happened.

I didn't appear to be hurt anywhere as far as I could tell, though the ropes were tied awful tight and the ground was cold. Weasel's wound appeared to be hurting him something terrible. The jug, I figured, held whiskey to dull the pain.

Watching Weasel cut and swear and drink, I thought about how Ezra's throwing stick must have made him shoot himself. I almost laughed out loud thinking about it, but I stopped myself in time. Weasel looked over at me suddenly and caught me with my eyes open.

"So, boy, you're awake, are ya? Well, well. Welcome to my humble home."

He began to laugh, and the laugh turned into a cough. From the funny, slow sound of his voice, I figured he'd had more than a few sips from the jug already.

"Not speakin', eh? If you're waitin' for that Injun-lovin' friend of yours to rescue you, you can forget it. In case you didn't notice, he had a little run-in with me before. Or didn't he tell you about it?"

There was a pause, followed by a whoop of laughter.

"I said, didn't he *tell* you about it?"

He laughed again, then stopped short and said, "What's the matter, boy? Cat got *your* tongue, too? Hoo-eee! Just call me the cat!"

His cruel jokes made me fill up with anger, but I stayed quiet. Weasel kept right on talking.

"Someday you'll thank me for takin' ya away from

that scum, Ezra Ketcham. Famous guvment Injun fighter—ha!" Weasel spat into the fire.

It was the first I'd heard Ezra's full name. I wanted to know more, and Weasel went on. I reckon it was the whiskey making his tongue loose.

"He wasn't always the low-life scum he is now. When the guvment sent us out here to wipe out them savages, we were the best there was. We did the job, boy, yessir. Our orders were to *remove* them redskins, and that's what we did. Now, mind you, some of our men thought that meant we were supposed to move them Injuns to some other place. But Ezra and me, we knew what it meant. We removed 'em, all right, once and for all. We had us some fine times back in them days."

Weasel left off digging for the bullet, and his eyes stared away somewhere. I figured he was seein' all those fine times he'd had. Then his face changed, and he stabbed the knife hard into the dirt floor.

"And then that no-good Ketcham goes soft on me, goes plumb crazy! Starts talking about how the Injuns belong here more than us, how we got no right to drive them off and kill them like animals. They *are* animals, I tell him. But he don't listen anymore; he's gone plumb crazy."

Weasel's voice filled with mockery. "Then he takes up with a squaw—a *squaw*! Tells me to leave him alone, he wants to live with the Shawnees and be their brother. Builds an Injun house. Says the squaw's his wife and is going to give him a son. A half-breed animal, I told him. It should be killed!"

Weasel's face was twisted up like a fist, and his hand clenched the knife and pulled it from the earth. He held the knife in midair and continued speaking, his voice filled with loathing.

"He said he was glad his child would have Shawnee blood. Said he was ashamed of his white man's blood, ashamed of what the white man, what *we*, had done. I wasn't about to listen to that!"

Breathing heavily, his eyes squinted, Weasel slashed the knife through the air. "I cut out his tongue, and while he watched like the helpless worm he's turned into, I killed his squaw and the half-breed animal growing inside her!"

His eyes opened and fell on me. "So if you think, boy, that Ezra Ketcham will come here to rescue you, you'd best think again. I know he's got your daddy. What do I care? I got the rifle, that's all I wanted. Find a man with his leg stuck in a trap, and a perfectly good rifle layin' beside him, now what would you do? A man'd have to be a fool not to take it, and I ain't nobody's fool. Don't look at me like that, boy. Ya ought to be grateful. I coulda killed him. As it is, I got a horse and a mule, some li'l ole pigs and some chickens, too. Now, that ain't half bad. And I got you, of course."

Weasel took a long pull on the whiskey jug, all the while looking me over real good. He set down the jug and wiped his hand across his mouth. "Now I just gotta decide what I'm gonna do with you."

11

I DIDN'T much like the way Weasel was staring at me. It reminded me of the look in Gideon Thurstan's eyes when he'd come to help us at slaughtering time. He'd size up each pig with a long look, so as to decide which one out of the bunch would get its throat cut that day.

I didn't aim to wait around to have my throat cut, and I didn't much want to find out what other ideas Weasel might come up with. But I felt as helpless as a pig led to slaughter, hog-tied as I was on the floor.

I watched Weasel take another big drink out of the jug, and it gave me an idea. No man could drink as much as Weasel had been drinking without having to answer a call of nature. So far I hadn't said a word, so as not to take a chance on making Weasel mad, but now I blurted, "I need to go out."

Weasel stared at me dumbly.

"To the privy," I explained.

Weasel laughed and mimicked me, "To the privy, you say? Well, ain't you the fancy one. Well, there's no 'privy' here, boy. You gotta go, you pick any bush you like the look of. Not a bad idea, at that," he mumbled, staggering to his feet. He let out a terrible curse as he put weight down on his shot foot.

I waited, still tied, as Weasel lurched toward the cabin door, his hands fumbling with the front of his trousers.

"I reckon you'll need to untie me," I said.

Weasel stopped for a moment, closing one eye and pinning me with the other. "You don't aim to try anything stupid, do ya, boy?"

"No, sir," I answered, trying to sound respectful. "I just have to go real bad."

Weasel picked up Pa's rifle, carried it over, and set it down next to him while he tried to untie my legs, swearing at the knots. Finally, growing impatient, he cut through the ropes with his knife, picked up the rifle, and said, "Go on with ya."

"I'll need my hands, too," I said, just as meekly as I could.

Weasel slashed through the ropes that tied my hands and watched scornfully as I forced my cramped legs and arms to move. He pushed me toward the door with the point of the rifle. Both of us were stumbling, but for different reasons.

Outside Weasel kept the rifle pointed at me as he relieved himself in the underbrush. I tried to linger as long as I could, taking in every detail of my surroundings. It was still dark, but in one direction I could see a brightening in the sky. That was east.

To my right, I heard a familiar nicker and saw the faint outline of Job and, nearby, Crabby. They were tied up, not fenced. I wondered if Weasel had tended to them at all since he'd taken them.

Weasel pushed me roughly with the point of the gun, and I headed inside again, where he gave me a sudden shove that sent me sprawling back to the floor.

He swore as he picked up the short pieces that were left of the rope I had been tied with, and threw them to the floor in disgust. They were no good now for tying me up, and I wondered what Weasel would do. His eyes were red rimmed and glassy from pain, and the whiskey had made him mean and impatient and clumsy.

Weasel's head swung drunkenly as he searched the room for something to tie me with. He grabbed some pieces of dirty cloth and used them to fasten me to a chair, the only piece of furniture in the room other than the crude table. His hands shook as he struggled with the knots.

"Ya ain't goin' far with a chair tied to yer back," he said, seeming quite pleased with himself. I tried to look just as helpless and scared as a rabbit. It wasn't hard. I was as scared as I'd ever been, and I must have looked pretty helpless, lying sideways on the floor, tied up to a chair.

Then Weasel grabbed a pile of old animal skins that I figured he used for a bed, dragged them over in front of the door, and lay down on them heavily. His back was propped against the cabin door; Pa's rifle was on his lap, pointing my way. Casting one bloodshot eye at me, he muttered, "I wouldn't move if I was you, boy," and closed his eyes.

I didn't even think about moving for a long time. I just watched Weasel and tried to puzzle out what to do next. I thought of the first time I had seen Weasel. We were headed west to Ezra's place, and Weasel was headed in the opposite direction, though on the same side of the big river. Pa had said Weasel was a creature of the night, and I reckoned he had been going home to sleep as the sun came up. If I was right, I was now somewhere east of Ezra's. If I could escape, I wouldn't waste any time trying to figure out which way to go. I'd head west and hope I'd soon find familiar territory.

I watched Weasel and waited. Finally his breathing was deep and regular. His mouth dropped open, and his fingers loosened on the rifle. Without making any noise or sudden movement, I began to test my bonds.

I was lying on my side, my hands tied to the top crosspiece of the chair, above my head, my feet spread and tied separately to the two front legs of the chair. It wasn't exactly comfortable.

At first I concentrated on my hands. As Weasel had tied the knots, I'd pushed against the tightening of them as much as I dared, hoping to gain myself some slack. I figured it was harder to tighten up on a knot made with bulky cloth than one made with rope, and it looked like I was right. Now every time I pushed against the knots I gained some room. My hands were still small—not like Pa's, so big and rough and knobby from hard work—so I didn't need much.

Finally my hands slipped free. I blessed whiskey for addling a man's wits and making him careless.

I felt strange, calm, and cold, as I inched my hands ever so carefully down to the knots holding my feet, keeping an eye on Weasel all the time.

After I got my legs untied, I lay quietly on the

floor, wiggling my fingers and toes to work the cramps out of my muscles before I tried to move. I wanted to be ready.

Ready for what? I asked myself. Where could I go? There were no windows in the cabin. Some of the chinks between the logs were wide, sure enough, but not big enough to slip through. And Weasel sat in front of the door.

The sight of him with Pa's gun, stolen while Pa was caught helplessly in a trap, made me feel even more cold and calm, almost like it wasn't even me, like I was watching myself.

I stood up, made sure all my parts were working, and walked across the room without making a sound. Standing at Weasel's feet, I told myself not to think about what I was about to do. Just do it, I told myself. It's your only chance.

Leaning down, I put my hands on the gun, my left hand on the barrel, my right hand near the trigger, and pulled hard. Weasel's hands tightened on the rifle and his eyes flew open, staring into mine with a crazy, startled look.

Being as I was standing up and fully awake, it wasn't too hard to reach down and wrest the gun from Weasel's grasp. He bellowed like an animal and tried to struggle to his feet.

I'd never pointed a gun at a human being before,

but I didn't think twice. I held it on Weasel and said, "I'm leaving now. Move away from the door and don't try to stop me."

My voice sounded high and shaky and I knew what I must look like to Weasel. His face began to twist into a grin, and he started to speak, but I cut him off.

"It would be a pleasure to kill you with my pa's gun," I said.

Weasel looked confused, like maybe he wasn't sure if he was awake or dreaming. He began to slide away from the door, dragging the skins across the dirt floor beneath him.

I kicked the door open, keeping the gun pointed at Weasel's chest. My fingers twitched at the trigger as I thought of Ezra, his wife and unborn baby, and of Pa, caught in Weasel's trap. Trembling, I tore my eyes from Weasel's gaze and ran out the door. A hand shot out, grabbed my leg, and held on. I nearly fell, but, recovering, I stomped down hard on the arm with my other foot and ran blindly toward where I had seen Job tied.

Still holding the gun, I untied the horse and climbed on. No saddle, no blanket, no reins. It didn't matter. "C'mon, old boy," I shouted, digging my heels into his flanks, and off we flew, heading west, as the sun rose in the east.

As we crashed through the brush, I heard Crabapple braying furiously at being left behind. Weasel could never catch us on the old mule, and from the curses that followed us, I reckoned he knew it.

12

JOB and I charged wildly through the forest, headed in what I could only hope was the direction of Ezra's place. I didn't care right at first which way we were going. I only cared about putting distance between me and Weasel. It seemed like Job felt the same way.

After a while, I slowed Job to a walk. Wrapping my arms around his neck, I let my face fall into the damp, comforting warmth of his mane. I stayed that way until the shivers that were coming from someplace deep inside me stopped. Then I lifted my face and looked around.

The forest was quiet, except for an occasional burst of bird song. I kept listening, and soon I could hear the faint, continuous murmur of the Ohio River. For a moment I felt surprised that the river was still flowing along, unaware of my predicament and uncaring. Job picked up the scent of water, pricked up his ears, and moved forward eagerly.

I could feel myself relax. The big river flowed westward. All I had to do was follow it, and I'd soon come to some place I knew. I was grateful to Job for his steadiness, for all of a sudden I was so tired it was all I could do to sit upright. I slumped against Job's neck and let him take me toward the river.

After a drink and a rest, I set Job on a path slightly up and away from the snags and rocks of the river bank. We picked our way along until the river narrowed and the sides steepened. Soon we were heading off a bit north toward Ezra's.

I never saw him coming, but suddenly Ezra was standing in front of us. The look on his face was a picture: worry, relief, and gladness all mixed together. I slid down off Job and ran to Ezra, flinging myself against him before I even knew what I was doing. We stood that way for I don't know how long. Ezra patted my back, making a soothing sound over and over again, "Umm-hmm . . . umm-hmm . . . umm-hmm . . ." Then he lifted me onto Job's back, and we walked the rest of the way through the forest together.

A S we approached the we-gi-wa, Molly ran out to greet us, crying, "Nathan! You're alive! I knew you were, I knew it. Come see Papa. He's better!"

Pa was sitting up in his bed of skins, looking almost like his old self. He hugged me hard, then held me by my shoulders and looked into my face and smiled. He said quietly, "I'm right glad you're back, son." All the things I wanted to say got stuck in a big ball in the back of my throat and stayed there. It seemed like Pa was having the same trouble. "Better get yourself some food," he said finally. "Ezra's taking care of Job."

When I had eaten one bowl of stew and was commencing on the second, Molly begged me to tell about my trip back home. Between bites, I retraced my steps with words. When I got to the part about finding Miz Tizz and the chickens slaughtered, I saw Pa's face darken and Ezra's twist up in that way that made him look so fearsome. Molly crawled onto Pa's lap. I felt real bad making her cry. Just telling about it was like it was happening all over again, and I realized I was crying, too.

I knew I'd done the right thing to bury Miz Tizz when I saw the look on Pa's face and the way he nodded his head just the slightest bit.

When I told about Weasel stalking me in the dark, I could feel all their eyes on me, wide and wondering. "So I reached into my pack and pulled out your— your whatchamacallit, Ezra—and threw it right at his middle where he was holding Pa's gun." Ezra let out a whoop and banged his fist on his knee. I'd never seen him so fired up. Molly cried, "Nathan! You didn't!" and Pa shushed everyone so I could go on.

By the time I got to the part about Weasel swearing at me cause his foot was shot, Ezra was laughing so hard there were tears rolling down his face. I was starting to enjoy myself, feeling like a real storyteller, the way Ezra was carrying on and Pa and Molly were exclaiming and shaking their heads.

But then I began to tell the final part where I walked past Weasel and out the door, and all at once I felt the coldness in my chest again, the tightness around my mouth, the hardness in my heart. "I wanted to kill him," I said softly. Then I was shouting, "I hate him! I wish I did kill him! Someday I will kill him, I will!"

Silence filled the we-gi-wa. Molly was looking at me in a puzzled way, like I was a stranger. I tried to make them understand what had happened, how I felt. "He told me about you, Ezra—about you and fighting

the Shawnees and about your wife and . . . the baby."
Looking into Ezra's eyes and frozen face, I thought,
He feels this way, too, like something's cold and dead
inside. We're the same now, Ezra and me. There was
a bitter taste in my mouth. I swallowed.

Pa cleared his throat and said, "Nathan, you've
had a bad time, but it's over now. What you need is
a good, long rest." Then he added softly, "I'm very
proud of you, son."

I was glad to sink into the bed, to surround myself
with the smells of wool and tanned leather, to turn
away from the others. I couldn't face the wary look
in Molly's eyes, the worry behind Pa's, the knowing
in Ezra's. As I drifted off to sleep, I heard Pa's words
again: "I'm very proud of you, son." I had imagined
him saying those words to me and imagined how good
I'd feel. But now it was really happening, and I didn't
feel good. I felt ashamed. I had the chance to kill
Weasel and didn't. Why didn't you just pull the trigger? I asked myself over and over again. I could have
come back and told Ezra, I got revenge for your wife
and your baby. I could have told Pa and Molly, Weasel
won't be hurting folks anymore. I could have rescued
Crabby, too. Instead all I did was save my own skin.

We passed several days in the we-gi-wa, for me to
rest and for Pa to gather his strength for the trip
home. His leg was fine, he said, as good as new, and

he made a lot of fuss over Molly's skill at healing. I could tell she was pleased. I was glad Pa was better, and I wanted to join in the jokes and stories and games like I used to. But something wouldn't let me. I sat, as silent as Ezra, brooding about Weasel. I knew I was making everyone jittery, but I couldn't help myself.

Weasel haunted me as he haunted Ezra, as he had haunted my dreams as a little boy. Only before he was just make-believe. He'd been scary, but almost fun scary to imagine. Now he was too real. I kept picturing him laughing when he spoke of Ezra and Pa, laughing at me. Then I'd imagine him lying by the door, wondering if I'd kill him or not. Why didn't I just pull the trigger? Over and over again, the scene passed through my mind. I could feel myself squeezing the trigger. You think I can't kill you, Weasel, but you'll see, I thought. You'll see.

Looking at Pa and Molly laughing and joking, I'd think, How can they joke when Weasel is still out there, when he could come back to hurt us? They acted like everything was the same as before. But nothing was the same. Pa was supposed to take care of things, to make things right. Now everything was wrong, and Pa didn't even seem to care. Such thinking made me feel disloyal to Pa, and that only made me feel worse.

My day thoughts got all twisted up with my night-

mares as I slept and stared the days away. In my bad
dreams, Molly and Pa and Mama were on one side
of a river. It was the side of everything good. Pa and
Mama were joking, and Molly was playing with the
dogs. I was on the other side of the river, where there
was hate and killing, and everything was dark and
mean and frightening. Weasel was there, and Ezra,
too, his face twisted up and sad. Ezra and I wanted
to cross the river, but no matter how hard we tried,
we couldn't get to the other side.

13

THE day came for us to leave the we-gi-wa and go back home. Pa was to ride Job so as to take it easy on his leg, and Duffy and Winston and Molly and me would walk along beside. We'd leave early to give ourselves plenty of time, Pa said.

It was early November, and the first snow of the winter was falling as we packed our few belongings and placed a blanket over Job's back for Pa to ride on. The dogs ran about excitedly, biting at the snow and sniffing the cold, moist air. Job pranced, his ears forward, eager to be off. Pa, looking big and healthy again, his cheeks red from the cold, snowflakes catching in his whiskers, stamped noisily about making last-minute preparations, and Molly, too, was flushed with the excitement of returning home.

But I didn't want to leave. I didn't want to leave Ezra, and, besides, there was something bothering me. "Pa," I began, "Weasel's still got Crabapple. He's got your saddle, too. It's—it's not right. We should go get them back."

Pa stopped working on the ropes he was tying and gave me a long look. At last he said, "Nathan, do you think it would be right to take Molly and head off into a situation like that?"

"No, sir," I said, "but he shouldn't have Crabby. He shouldn't even be allowed to live—not after all the things he's done. Why, you and me and Ezra, we could sneak up on him—he sleeps during the day mostly—and kill him. We could get back Crabby and your saddle and . . . And everything would be all right again," I finished lamely.

"Would it?" asked Pa softly, holding his head sideways and looking at me like he was really thinking about it. "I'll tell you what I think, Nathan. I think killing Weasel wouldn't change much at all, except for maybe bringing us closer to being like him. He's the one's got to answer for what he's done. For my part, I'm going to leave him behind. I'm sorry to lose Crabby. She's a good worker, bless her stubborn little

71

ears. But I'm going to buy a new mule and a new saddle and I'm going to go home with you and Molly and try to be happy like your mama would want us to do. I want you to try to do the same, son."

"But what about what Weasel did to you?" I asked. "What about what he did to Ezra and Ezra's family? How can you just forget it?"

"I'm not saying I'll forget about it. But I can't dwell on it. Life's full of sadness, Nathan, like your mama dying, and what Weasel did to Ezra's kin. There's more sadness in that than you and I have got tears to cry for it. But life's full of good things, too. I've still got my leg, haven't I? I've got you and Molly and a whole life ahead, God willing. If I forget all the good things to think about Weasel, then I'm letting him do something worse to me than what he's done already. I might as well have died there in that trap."

"What do you mean, Pa? We've *got* to think about Weasel!"

"Don't get me wrong, Nathan. I'll do everything I can to protect us. I just can't dwell on it."

"But what about Ezra?"

"Ezra's got to do what's right for him." Pa turned away and went back to tying his knots.

I turned away, too, feeling more confused and angry than ever. What about what's right for me? I thought. Nobody cares about that.

Everything was ready, but suddenly no one seemed in a hurry to leave. Ezra fussed with a strip of hide on the side of the we-gi-wa, Pa fidgeted with the reins he'd rigged up for Job, Molly scratched Duffy's ears. At last Pa walked over to Ezra and said, "Ezra, I'll never forget what you did—saving my life and bringing my children here, caring for them like you did. I'll never be able to thank you, either. I know—well, I know it wasn't an easy thing for you to do, getting mixed up with folks again and all. . . ." Pa faltered and didn't seem to know what to say next. "If we could ever help you out, you know where we are. And, if you took the notion, we'd be proud to have you visit with us."

Pa put out his hand, and Ezra shook it. Molly ran over and wrapped her arms around Ezra's legs. "Ezra, do! Come see us! Please!"

Ezra leaned over and picked Molly up. He hugged her for a minute, then set her down. He reached up and lifted the string of blue glass beads from around his neck and placed them around Molly's neck. He smiled at her, and for a moment I could imagine him, in this very place, smiling at his wife and his own child. Then the other look, the still sadness, came back to his face.

It was my turn to say good-bye. But I had no words for what was between Ezra and me. We were joined, like in my dreams, by our hatred of Weasel. I could feel it burning in Ezra as it burned in me. We shook hands and I turned to go. When I looked back, he was gone.

We walked through the softly falling snow without speaking. The forest wrapped itself quietly in a blanket of whiteness as we headed home.

14

THAT night, when Job was fed and stabled in the barn, and a fire was burning in the wood stove, Molly touched the blue glass beads around her neck and asked, "Papa, it makes me sad to think of Ezra alone. Will he visit us?"

"I don't know, sugarplum," said Pa, "but I doubt he will. Not so's we'll see him, anyway."

"What do you mean?" I asked.

"Well," said Pa, "you and Molly never knew this, but Ezra was part of our lives long before this ever happened."

"How?" we asked.

Pa answered, "It's a long story, about Ezra. I reckon it's time you heard the whole thing. . . ."

He was quiet for a while, deciding how to start out, I guessed.

"In a peculiar kind of way, what happened to Ezra is our fault," he began.

"Our fault! What do you mean?" I cried, stunned.

"Oh, not yours and Molly's and mine, exactly," said Pa, "but all of us settlers'. We wanted to come west, to find cheap, new land and make it our own. We didn't give much thought to the folks who already lived here and always had. . . ."

"You mean the Shawnees, Pa?" I asked.

"Yes, and the Delawares and the Mingoes and the others who lived and hunted here. But long before we came, there were other white folks—frontiersmen, hunters, and trappers and such. Did you know that Daniel Boone himself was captured by Shawnees not far from here?"

"Daniel Boone? Really, Pa?" Molly and I had heard many stories about Daniel Boone on our trips to town. The men sitting around at the store would get to talking about old Daniel Boone and how he was the greatest, bravest frontiersman of all. Sometimes it seemed like there was no end to the tales about him, and each one topped the one that came before. Me and the other boys would listen until we were about ready to bust with the excitement of it. We'd run off to play Daniel Boone and the Indians. If Colin Whitefield was around, and he usually was since his pa owned the store, he got to be Daniel Boone 'cause he was biggest and strongest. The rest of us were Indians who mostly got killed off by the great Mr. Boone.

"What happened?" asked Molly.

"He must have escaped," I answered her. Daniel Boone always made daring escapes in the stories they told about him.

"Not this time," Pa chuckled. "The way I heard it, and this was from a white man who lived a long time with the Shawnees, Boone led a hunting party into Shawnee hunting grounds in 1769."

"That's"—Molly figured in her head—"seventy years ago!" she announced proudly.

"Right. Well, Boone and his men began killing all the game they could shoot, only they took just the furs and hides, leaving the meat to rot. Now, this was not the Shawnee way. They believed in using every part of the animal and wasting nothing. They captured Boone."

"What did they do to him, Pa?" I asked. In our games, Colin Whitefield always made the Indians do horrible, cruel things to their captives.

"They made Boone lead them to the camps of his men. They surprised the camps and took all the hides,

77

furs, guns, ammunition, horses, and anything else the white men might use for carrying out their expedition. Then, after warning them never to return, the Shawnees freed them and sent them home unharmed. But with what was the Shawnees' usual generosity, they gave each captive two pairs of moccasins, a doe-skin, a gun, and a few loads of powder so they wouldn't starve on their way back. What do you think of that?"

"They were nice, Papa," said Molly.

"I reckon Daniel Boone never came back after that," I said. "He must have been grateful to the Shawnees."

"Oh, but that's where you're wrong, Nathan," said Pa. "Instead of being grateful, Boone and his men were outraged at being treated that way. Their only thought was to return and get revenge, which they did. And other frontiersmen, hearing about the forests full of game, followed. The Shawnees must have thought there was a never-ending supply of white men, and, come to think of it, there was. The frontiersmen kept coming, followed by settlers who began building their fences and cabins. Indians who didn't like it were killed. Some attacked the settlements. The settlers cried for protection, and the government began its war on the Shawnees in earnest."

"Is that when Weasel and Ezra came here?" I asked, remembering Weasel's story.

"Well, the Indian wars went on for many years but, yes, Weasel and Ezra were sent here by the army, oh, probably fifteen years ago."

Pa paused for a while and stared off into the fire. "Then your ma and I heard that the Ohio territory was safe for settlers. We decided to come here and start a new life. We were young and strong and ready to work hard, and we did. We cleared the land and built our little cabin, and soon you were born, Nathan, and then Molly. They were good years. We were happy. We didn't think much about the Shawnees and how they got pushed out to make room for us. It was just the way of things.

"Then one day when Molly was just a baby, all of us went to town in the wagon. We needed a few supplies, but mostly we wanted to visit with folks, and your mama wanted to show off the baby. When we got there, the whole town was buzzing. What a to-do!"

"What about, Pa?"

"Well, the hostilities with the Shawnees had all but stopped, leastways near us, and Congress had passed something they called the Removal Act. The Shawnees who were left were to be removed to Kansas, some of them, and others to Oklahoma."

"What does it mean, 'removed to Kansas'?" Molly asked.

"It meant the Shawnees had to pick up and go where the government told them to go, live where they were told to live. And a great many of them did. They were accompanied by the government enforcement agents. But many of them died along the way. The journey was full of hardships, and the men who took them were the same men who had been killing Indians for years. They didn't put much value on the life of a Shawnee."

I thought of the we-gi-wa, and Ezra's wife. "But not all the Shawnees left," I said. "What about Ezra's wife?"

"That's what the town was buzzing about," Pa answered. "It seems one of the government's Indian fighters had quit the army, refusing to have any more part of fighting Indians or removing them anywhere. He had taken a Shawnee wife and was leaving with her to take up living on land he said belonged to the Shawnees forever, no matter what the government said. Folks just didn't know what to make of it! There were those as said that if she didn't leave peacefully with the others, she ought to be shot, and him along with her for deserting his army post. Other folks said that maybe it wasn't right to just up and kill a white man, an army man at that, or his wife, either, even if she was, as they said, only a squaw. Everybody had an opinion about it, but nobody knew what to do.

While the talk went back and forth, the man and his wife just up and started walking out of town. Nobody tried to stop 'em, either. But a lot of folks yelled ugly things after them as they left."

"The man was Ezra, wasn't it?" I asked.

"Yes," replied Pa.

"But you said Ezra was a part of our lives, Papa," said Molly. "What did you mean?"

"Well," continued Pa, "your mama was upset by the mood in the town and all the ugliness and shouting. She asked me to turn the wagon around and go on back home. She didn't much feel like visiting, and the supplies could wait. So we turned around, and soon we overtook Ezra and the woman. They kept walking, staring straight ahead, not glancing our way. I thought it was probably the right thing to just leave them be, but your mama noticed that the woman looked like she was going to have a baby. Your mama, having just had you, Molly, was noticing such things, I reckon, for it wasn't obvious to me. She called to them to ride in the wagon with us as far as our place. At first they wouldn't look our way, not trusting us to be friendly, and no wonder about that. But your mama kept talking, and soon they joined us in the wagon.

"Ezra wasn't much of a talker, even then," Pa said, smiling ruefully. "We introduced ourselves and he said their names, and that was about it. He said her name in Shawnee, and said it meant 'Gives-light-as-she-walks,' and I remember thinking that was real pretty. She fussed over you two a bit, but pretty much we rode in silence. There was a sadness about what they were doing that made it hard to talk about everyday things.

"When we got to our cabin, we asked them in for a rest and some food, but they said, no, they'd go on. They thanked us. Then Ezra said, 'I don't have much use for white folks anymore. But you were kind.' And then they were gone."

"Did you ever see them again, Papa?" asked Molly.

"No," said Pa, "but some time after that we began finding things."

"Finding things? Like what, Pa?" I asked.

"Do you remember the moccasins your mama used to wear sometimes?"

We nodded, picturing the soft leather slippers with the intricate designs made of beads and what Mama had told us were porcupine quills.

"You probably don't recollect the rattle you had as a baby, Molly, but I'll bet you remember a doll you had with fringed hair and a red cloth dress. The body was made of hide. You loved that doll, took it everywhere with you. Until Duffy—or maybe it was Win, I don't rightly recollect—chewed it up one day.

All the stuffing came out, fluff from a ripe cattail, I think it was. You cried and cried."

"I remember," said Molly softly.

"There was your whistle, Nathan, made from an eagle bone, and other things, gifts of food, a doe-skin . . ." Pa's voice drifted off.

"Ezra brought them?" Molly asked. "And Gives-light-as-she-walks?"

"We never knew for certain. That is, we never saw them leave the things. But we knew it was them. It was almost spooky sometimes, how we'd find something just when we needed it, like some proper leather when Crabby's harness was broke, some seed corn once when I couldn't get any. It was like they watched over us—sometimes I thought I could feel Ezra out there. All that summer and into the fall, the gifts mysteriously appeared."

"Where did you find them, Pa?" I asked.

"They were always left out in the stone wall I made when I cleared the land for the farm. Little things were tucked in a hollow between the rocks. We never knew when they would come. Your mama left a letter once, saying thank you and please stop in. It was there for a few weeks, and then it disappeared. They never did stop in, but she was glad they knew we were grateful. Then the gifts stopped. We didn't mind that, but we worried. Your ma fretted and fussed, wondering if something had gone wrong with the birthing of the baby, which she figured was due by then. Then we made a trip to town one day and heard folks talking.

"An Indian fighter they called Weasel had been in town bragging about killing a squaw. He said he'd fixed that 'white Injun' so he couldn't take the part of savages against honest, civilized folks. We heard it, and we knew who was meant."

Pa paused for a long time. Neither Molly nor I said a word.

" 'Course, we didn't realize then what he'd done to Ezra to keep him quiet. Weasel was a big hero then to a lot of folks. But that didn't last. You heard the stories yourselves of what Weasel did, how he began to prey upon the townsfolk and settlers, stealing and killing and such. I always believed I could protect you from such things—"

Pa broke off, shaking his head. His face, weathered and deeply lined, looked old in the flickering light from the fire.

"Anyway, for a long time nothing was left in the stone wall. Stories began to spread about a wild hermit who lived in a cave in the woods. People said he was crazy with grief, and that he used Shawnee magic so that anyone who came near his hideout would sicken and die. They said all sorts of other things, too ridiculous to repeat. Your mama and I didn't believe all the nonsense, but we knew the hermit was Ezra, and she couldn't bear to think of him out there, alone and sad."

Pa stopped again to smile at Molly. "You're a lot like your mama," he said. Then he continued. "She hoped he was gone, that he'd left to find his wife's people. She thought that if he couldn't abide the white man's ways, maybe he'd be able to be happy with the Shawnees.

"Then your mama got sick. I don't know how Ezra knew it. But one day I found some medicine left out on the wall, and I knew that Ezra was still watching out for us. It was too late to save your mama, of course. . . ." Pa sighed. "And then I heard and saw nothing of Ezra again until the day I woke up in his house with my leg sewed up and Molly spooning tea down my throat."

"How did you get there, Pa?" I still hadn't heard the whole story.

"I reckon Ezra carried me. I'd been walking along a game trail, when I stepped right into a trap. Big enough for a full-size bear, it was, and I never even saw it. That trap was hidden so carefully, more carefully, I can see now, than it had to be to snare an animal. The pain was fierce, and I was trying to figure what to do when a man came toward me out of the woods. I couldn't believe my good fortune. I called out to him with a glad greeting. I'll never forget the way he looked at me. Like I was just another trapped animal—no, less than that, even. He picked up my rifle where I'd dropped it when I fell and he said, 'Leastways ya got a decent rifle.' He found my knife, ran his finger over the blade, and took that, too. Then he turned around and left me there to die. Right then and there, I knew who he was.

"I lay there kind of stunned for a while. I figured out he must set the trap like that on purpose, not caring what he caught, animals or folks. He'd just take what he wanted either way.

"So there I was, thinking I was going to die, knowing you two were here alone. I thought I'd go crazy thinking about it. I was there at least a day before Ezra found me, because I remember it turning dark and light and dark again, but I was getting pretty fuzzy from the pain, and it could have been longer. I dug out the trap from where it was buried in the ground and walked a ways with it, but it tore at my leg too bad. And—that's all I remember."

"Oh, Papa," mumbled Molly, climbing up on his lap, "don't tell any more tonight."

"You're right, sugarplum," said Pa. "That's enough for one night. But at least there's a happy ending. Here we are, safe and sound, thanks to Ezra."

"But it's not a happy ending for Ezra," I said.

"No," said Pa sadly, "it's not. I wish I knew how to change that. But I think the kindest thing we can do is to leave the poor man in peace. That's all he asks, to be left alone."

"Papa," said Molly sleepily, "I don't think anyone really wants to be alone. Do they?" Her voice slowed and stopped as she fell asleep against Pa's shoulder.

He stood up, holding Molly in one strong arm and putting the other around me. "Come on, Nathan, it's time we all turned in. I'm sorry, son. That wasn't much of a bedtime story, was it?"

"It's all right, Pa," I said.

But it wasn't all right. All night I tossed and turned, thinking about everything that Pa had told us. First I lay shivering with sorrow for Ezra and his wife and all the Shawnee people, with fear for Pa, lying helpless in the trap. Then I threw off the quilts, burning with hatred for Weasel. I know what I can do for Ezra, Pa, I thought. If I kill Weasel, he'll be able to be happy again. And so will I.

15

ONE day the wind was howling around the corners of the cabin, blowing the snow so fast there were no single flakes, just a whirl of white outside the window. I was sitting by the fire, thinking, as usual, about my plan to kill Weasel. Molly sat at the table, writing.

I'll ask Pa if I can borrow the gun to do some hunting, I thought. He'd been watching me awful careful lately, and I knew he'd never let me go far in the harsh winter weather by myself. I'd wait till spring, when the weather broke and Pa was busy with plowing. I'd ask if I could go out to the stand of hickory trees on the ridge to see if I could shoot a squirrel. I'd slip away, find Weasel's cabin, sneak up on him, and kill him. "This is for Ezra," I'd say before I shot him, "and for his wife, and for my pa." Then I'd get Crabapple and come on home. Then, at last, the awful tightness around my chest would go away.

Molly interrupted my planning. "Would you read this, Nathan?" she asked, handing me the paper she'd been working on. I read:

Dear Ezra,
I hope you find this letter. Pa told us about
the stone wall. He says you want to be alone
and we should leave you be. But I think it
must be sad to be alone. Pa says your wife's
kin went to Kansis. If you go there you could
find them and live how you want. Only not
alone. Please write back if you find this.

> Your friend,
> Molly Fowler

P.S. Pa's leg feels fine.
P.S. again. I made blue biskits too.

"It's a good letter, Molly," I said, handing it back to her. "Do you think he'll ever find it?"

"Yes," she answered, "I know he will. Sometimes I'm sure he's been out there, watching over us, like Papa said. Do you ever feel it, Nathan?"

"Yes," I said, surprised that Molly knew about the feeling I had of Ezra's nearness.

Molly took the paper and rolled it up tightly in a piece of tanned leather. I helped her rub oil into the leather so that the water couldn't get through, and stood by the door as she ran into the swirling snow and tucked the letter between two stones in the wall.

She went out to look in the wall every day of the rest of that long winter. In my own way, I was waiting for a sign from Ezra, too. I often hoped that some night, as we sat in the cabin, we'd hear the knock again, and Ezra would be standing outside the door. Sometimes I was so sure he was near, I'd stand outside, staring into the darkness, waiting for him to come forward. I imagined him beckoning to me again, and we would go off into the night—only this time we'd go to Weasel's cabin and kill him. I could feel Weasel out there, too, always. Weasel, Ezra, and me—the three of us all tangled up in something that wasn't finished yet. I made a promise to the dark winter sky: I'll finish it someday. Some day soon.

But I kept my thoughts about Weasel to myself. I wanted to say to Molly, Don't worry, I know what will make Ezra happy again, and I'm going to take care of everything. But when I talked like that about what was really on my mind, Pa would look worried, or worse, and lift an eyebrow at me as if to say, We'll see about that, young man! Like I was still a stupid little boy. He didn't understand at all.

One day Pa was mending harness when he looked up at me and said, "Nathan, I hate to see you wasting your time brooding about that no-good excuse for a human being."

"What?" I asked, startled. Could Pa read my mind? "Who?"

"You know who. You're thinking about Weasel again. I can see it on your face, plain as day."

As long as Pa had brought it up, I decided to ask him some things I'd been wondering about for a long time. "Pa," I began, "what would you have done if you were me?"

"What do you mean, son?" Pa asked, setting down the harness and looking at me close.

"At Weasel's cabin that night . . . you'd have killed him, wouldn't you? You wouldn't have just run like I did."

"Nathan, is that what's bothering you? That you didn't shoot Weasel when he was lying there half-drunk on the ground? You didn't need to kill him, son. All you had to do was to make him move so's you could get away."

"But what would *you* have done?" I asked again.

Pa pushed his lower lip out and pulled on his whiskers like he did sometimes when he was working on an idea. At last he said slowly, "I don't know, Nathan. I honestly don't know. It wasn't me there that night, so I can't say for sure. If I'd been angry enough, I might have. If I'd needed to kill him to get away, I'd have done it. But to just shoot him when he was lying there ... Well, I can't say."

"He's done worse to lots of others," I said.

"He has."

"So why shouldn't I have killed him? Why shouldn't I kill him now?"

"You did what you had to do that night, Nathan. You kept your wits about you. You escaped. It took a great deal of courage, don't you realize that?"

"But I—"

Pa interrupted me, something he didn't often do. "But nothing, Nathan. Where did you ever learn that pulling a trigger is what makes a man brave? Do you think you'd feel better about what happened to Ezra and his wife, and their baby, and all the others he's killed and hurt, if you'd shot him there on the ground that night?"

"Yes!" I shouted. "At least we'd have revenge!"

"Revenge," said Pa slowly. "I can see how you'd want revenge, Nathan, I can. But I don't think it would help you now. You may not believe this, but I think that if you had killed Weasel that night, or even some night since then, you'd still feel the way you're feeling now. You'd feel sorrow for Ezra and all the others, and killing Weasel wouldn't make it go away."

Suddenly Pa smiled. "If it's revenge you want, Nathan, think about this. How do you think Weasel feels about getting shot and outwitted by an eleven-year-old boy? How do you think the famous 'Injun fighter' feels about that? I bet he squirms every time he thinks of it!"

I felt my lips twitching into a smile, thinking about what Pa had said.

"Another thing, Nathan . . . killing a man lying helpless on the ground sounds like something Weasel would do. Seems to me what you did is much better. When I told you I was proud of you, Nathan, I meant it. Your ma would have been proud, too. I hope you'll get to where you can feel proud, also."

I didn't know what to say. The way Pa explained it, it made sense. But then when I thought about Weasel and all the things he'd done, it didn't make sense anymore.

"But, Pa," I said, "someone should stop him!"

"Oh, someone will," Pa answered. "Someday someone'll give him what he deserves, I reckon."

"Why not me?" I shouted.

"Nathan, it's not up to an eleven-year-old boy to do the killing of a man like Weasel."

"I'm almost twelve!" I said.

"Or a twelve-year-old boy, either." Pa went on, "And I don't aim to go taking foolish chances, not when I've got you and Molly to take care of. I won't do a thing that might leave you two alone again, do you understand, Nathan?"

"Yes, Pa," I answered.

And I did. Pa had me and Molly to worry about. Ezra had had a bellyful of killing and had turned his back on it. And Pa was dead set against me doing it. Who else was there?

"What about the law, Pa?" Even as I said it, I didn't know what I meant, not exactly. I'd heard some about the law, but I'd never actually seen any of it.

"That's a good question, Nathan," said Pa, pulling on his whiskers again. "There's a lot of talk about law in these parts, but you've probably noticed it isn't much more than talk. Law still belongs to the cities and towns. I believe we'll have law out here in the settlements someday, but until then we have to do the best we can on our own. I knew that when I came out here, so there's no sense in me feeling aggrieved about it now."

That night I lay in bed, staring into the blackness, thinking about everything Pa had said. I felt more confused than ever. Killing was wrong; everybody said so. But I kept coming back to the same thing, and it wouldn't go away: Weasel was still out there. He could come here and hurt us. He could be hurting other folks, even now. Maybe Pa could rest easy knowing that, but I couldn't. Maybe Pa could wait for the day when we'd have the law to take care of men like Weasel. But I couldn't.

16

SILENTLY I crept out of bed, dressed, and put on my coat, boots, hat, and gloves. I found Pa's gun and some bullets. I was going to find Weasel. Pa wouldn't like it, but hadn't he said we had to do the best we could on our own?

I was about to leave when I saw Molly's papers and pens on the table, and I decided to write a letter to Pa. But after a few starts, I crumpled the paper and threw it into the fire.

I didn't know myself what I was going to do, so how could I tell Pa?

I eased quietly out the door. It was late February, and we were having what Pa called "sucker spring."

That meant warm weather that tried to fool you into thinking winter was over. The snow was grainy and wet, so my footsteps made a squishy sound as I walked. The moon shining on the snow made the night seem almost as bright as day.

I had made the journey to Weasel's cabin so many times in my mind that I didn't hesitate about which way to go. For a minute I stopped to consider whether I ought to take Job. It would be a lot faster, and I'd have liked his company. But I felt bad enough about sneaking out without telling Pa, and if something happened to me I'd be leaving Molly and Pa without a gun or a horse. Better to walk, I decided.

The way I figured it, I'd get near Weasel's cabin and wait till daylight, when he'd most likely be sleeping. I'd sneak up and— And what? Kill a sleeping man?

I guess you'll know what to do when you have to do it, I told myself. Maybe it was true. All I really knew was that I had to do something. I had to go back.

I hurried on, trying to keep my mind empty. When the sky began to show bright in the east, I figured I was pretty close to Weasel's place. I stopped and hid myself in a thick stand of spruce trees, where I'd be out of the wind and safe from Weasel's eyes. No sense in meeting up with him as he made his way home.

It was hard to stay still, I was so jumpy. Every tree

branch scraping in the wind made me turn, expecting to see Weasel step right into my hiding place.

At last the day dawned, gray and solemn, and I figured Weasel would most likely be home by now and fixing to sleep. I came out and began walking slowly toward where I thought his cabin was. I didn't want any pesky crows or blue jays sounding off and warning Weasel that someone was coming, so I took my time. I had to circle back and around a few times, until there it was—Weasel's cabin.

I could feel my heart begin to thump as I remembered lying helpless on the floor while Weasel told his awful tales. I imagined the scene inside: Weasel asleep on his pile of filthy furs, not knowing I was sneaking up on him, just like he'd gone sneaking up on so many others. Keeping that thought in my mind, I crept closer. I had that same cold feeling as before, when I'd been trapped in the cabin, the coldness that shut out everything else but Weasel and what I had to do next. I was surprised to see that the door was open a crack. Holding my breath, I stepped forward to peer through the opening, sure I'd find myself face to face with Weasel.

Ppptr-rrrrrrr!

There was a sudden burst of sound as a grouse broke from the cover of a nearby tree in a flurry of beating wings, scaring me half out of my wits.

"*Aaaaahhh!*" My breath came rushing out in a cry of surprise. Then something dark and furry ran out the cabin door right past my feet. Screaming now, I fell backward into the snow, my gun flying out of my hands.

As my scream echoed through the forest, I waited for the door to open wide and for Weasel to say, So it's you again, boy—only this time ya ain't got a gun in your hand. . . .

But the echo died away, and a deep silence filled the woods. No one came to the door. Nothing moved. As I lay there, I remembered a silence like this. It was the day I had returned home to find the animals gone and Miz Tizz dead.

Slowly I came to see what I'd been too worked up to notice before. There were no footprints in the snow around the cabin, except for mine and some from small animals and birds. There was no smoke coming from the chimney. An awful feeling came over me then—I remembered that the cabin hadn't smelled real good before, but the stink coming from it now was about the worst I'd ever smelled.

I knew what it meant, and I wanted to turn and run from it as fast as I could. But I had to see what was in there. I had to know.

I made myself open the cabin door and step inside. I jumped as more small creatures went squeaking and scuttling into the dark corners. In the dim light, my eyes were drawn to the pile of skins that was Weasel's bed. Taking one step closer, I could see the form of a man huddled under the skins, or leastways what used to be a man. I couldn't see a face, or anything that looked human at all. But it was Weasel, all right. There was no doubt about that. The stream of light coming through the doorway fell on a tangle of matted brown hair and caught on a patch of pure white, making it stand out in the darkness clear as could be. Covering my mouth, I turned and began running through the snow.

I don't know how long I ran through the forest, choking and crying, feeling more alone than I'd ever felt in my life, and more scared. What I'd seen was too awful to think about. But it meant Weasel was dead. Weasel—dead. I couldn't take it in.

After a long time I stopped running and leaned, gasping, against a tree. I looked around and it came to me that without thinking about it I was heading for Ezra's house. It made me feel better to think I was near Ezra, and I kept on running till I thought my heart was going to burst wide open. And suddenly, like before, there was Ezra, coming toward me through the woods.

"Ezraaaa!" I cried.

Ezra ran to meet me. His strong arms pulled me

close and held me until I could stop my crying and shaking. He kept his arms around my shoulders while I wiped my face on my sleeve. Even then it was a while before I could tell him what had happened. When I was finished, I started crying and shivering all over again.

Ezra picked me right up and carried me to the we-gi-wa. He fed me and gave me something hot to drink, and wrapped me in blankets by the fire. I think I even slept a little. But when I woke up, Ezra was right there next to me.

"Ezra," I said. "Weasel . . . He's dead."

Ezra nodded.

"He must have— It looked like he died all by himself, in his bed." A sudden thought struck me. "Ezra . . . I wonder . . . Do you think Weasel might have died of poison? You know, from where he shot himself in the foot? If his leg got real bad, he would have been too sick to hunt, too sick to get food and water. . . ."

My voice dropped off as I thought about the way Weasel must have died. It was awful to think about. Alone, hurt, sick, hungry, and thirsty. The way Pa would have died, if Weasel had had his way.

"Pa said someday Weasel would get what he deserves," I said, and I sat there, thinking how strange it was, and how right, somehow.

After a while, Ezra got up and came back to the fire with something in his hands. It was a shovel. He stood looking at me, and all at once I understood. He meant for us to go back there, to the cabin. To bury Weasel.

At first I couldn't believe it. I never wanted to go back there, ever. And Ezra hated Weasel, too. Why would he want to bury him?

I tried to remember what Pa had said about burying. It seemed like it had more to do with the folks doing the burying than with who it was getting buried. Weasel was a savage, I thought, but we aren't. Ezra and me, burying Weasel . . . Somehow that seemed right, too. I got up from my place by the fire, and we followed my trail back to the cabin through the snow.

We chose a spot where the sun had warmed the ground a little, but even with that and the thaw we'd had, it was rough digging. We took turns, scraping more than digging the frozen earth until we made a shallow grave. Then we went inside, wrapped the skins around what was left of Weasel, and dragged the whole pile into the hole. After we filled in the dirt, we covered it with the biggest rocks we could carry, to keep the animals out.

Another grave, I thought. How many graves had to be dug because of you, Weasel?

I looked at Ezra. There were no tears at this burial,

no pretty words to say. It was over. Weasel was dead and buried. Are you happy now, Ezra? I wondered. Am I? All I could think of was how tired I felt.

Then I remembered Crabapple. There wasn't a sign of him anywhere. He must have run away, I decided. I imagined him running free and wild in the woods, doing as he pleased, and I smiled. Stubborn old Crabby. He probably liked it just fine.

Ezra and I turned away from Weasel's grave and walked into the forest together. Ezra stayed with me until we could see our cabin in the distance, and then he stopped.

"Wait, Ezra, please don't go yet. I have to get something," I said.

I ran to the stone wall and got Molly's letter and handed it to Ezra, saying, "It's from Molly. It would mean a lot to her if you'd write back. It would mean a lot to all of us to know how you're doing. We think about you all the time."

Ezra grasped the letter and both my hands in his. He looked at me and smiled. Then he stared off past me for a long moment. His eyes seemed to be looking at a new place, and I wished, like always, that I knew what he was seeing.

He squeezed my hands hard, then turned to go. I watched him disappear into the trees.

"Good-bye, Ezra," I called. "Good-bye."

PA could barely speak when he saw me. He was glad I was home safe and mad as a hornet at me for going, both at the same time.

"I didn't mean to worry you, Pa," I said. "It was just something I had to do. Weasel's dead."

From the look on his face, I knew he was afraid of what I'd done. "No, Pa," I said, "I didn't kill him."

I told Pa and Molly the whole story. It was strange. I had thought I'd feel so good when Weasel was dead, carefree and happy like before, but it wasn't like that. I felt different. Better mostly, I guess. But Pa was right. It didn't make the things Weasel had done go away, or the hurt of them. I still thought about Ezra at night and wished I could help him. And I had terrible dreams about Weasel's cabin and what I had seen there.

17

⎯⎯⎯⎯⎯⎯⎯⎯⎯⎯

THE March days followed one another, it seemed to me, without a clear notion about where they were heading. One day was warm and sunny with the smells of damp earth and worms and things coming alive, and the next day would come blowing and snowing and setting things right back to where they'd been. I expect it was like that every year, but I'd never found it so contrary before.

Pa and Molly didn't seem bothered by it. They were in high spirits, making plans for planting. Pa had let Molly order flower seeds, and she spent hours drawing pictures of Mama's garden, showing what she'd plant where and how it would look. Pa had spent the winter mending harness, fixing tools, and sharpening the plow blade, and he was itching to get started. And they talked all the time about the fiddle contest and dance that Colin Whitefield's daddy put on every year on the first day of April.

We used to go every year when Mama was alive, and it was about the most fun of the whole year. We didn't go last April 'cause we were mourning for Mama, but Pa was determined to go this year and see that we had a good time. Molly was busting her britches about it, but I, for my part, didn't much feel like singing and dancing.

We planned to leave early in the morning and stay, as Pa said, till the last tune was fiddled and the last dance was danced.

"Aren't you afraid of falling asleep on the way home, Pa?" Molly asked. "I always do."

Pa laughed and said, "We'll just have to count on Job to get us home. He knows the way better than I do in the dark."

THE first day of April dawned clear and warm. As the sun was rising, I went out to hitch Job up to the wagon. Molly came out after a while, in a new dress she had made for herself out of one of Mama's.

106

"You look real nice," I told her. She looked pleased, and surprised, too.

"Wish I could say the same for you, Nathan Fowler," she replied. "No girl's going to dance with you the way you look!"

I looked down at my trousers, which were too short, and my everyday shirt, and shrugged. What did I care how I was dressed? The only reason I was even going to the dumb dance was 'cause Pa would make me go, anyhow, even if I didn't want to. But I wasn't going to dance with any girls, no matter how much Molly teased.

Pa came out, looking real handsome with his dark hair and beard neatly trimmed. Next to his whiskers his shirt stood out clean and white. We led the wagon around front of the cabin and loaded in the basket full of biscuits, chicken, and preserves, the quilts for the ride home, and Pa's mouth harp so he could join in the music. I added some grain for Job, and we were on our way.

Pa let me drive the wagon, and I was glad it was Job and not Crabby doing the pulling, what with all the soft mud and swollen creek beds we had to go through. Job was full of beans after his winter in the barn, and I had to keep holding him back with a pull on the reins and a "Slow there, Job, steady now, boy, it's a long trip you've got to make."

"He knows he's going to a dance!" shouted Molly, and that got Pa going on a silly song about a horse who went to a dance and fell in love with a pig by mistake.

The air felt fine on my face, and the woods were full of the smells and sounds of spring. Red buds showed on most all the trees, and a fuzzy greenness surrounded the branches of the willows. Pa and Molly were in such fine spirits, I found myself joining in the singing and fooling. It seemed that all the creatures of the forest were forgetting to be cautious, too, now that spring had come at last. We stopped to watch a flock of turkeys so caught up in their courting games that they paid us no mind. The gobblers spread their fancy tail feathers and strutted about, showing them off for the hens, who were more interested in looking for bugs in the grass, as far as I could tell. "See, Molly, why bother getting all dressed up when the girls don't even notice!" I joked.

Orioles and blue jays and finches flew about, gathering sticks and grasses for their nests, and even the shyest creatures—the raccoons, groundhogs, foxes, and deer—were out sniffing the air and feeling the sun on their faces. I thought I knew how a bear must feel, coming out of his winter darkness into the light.

18

THE street in town was full of wagons and horses and children. Folks looking uncomfortable but proud in their fancy clothes were laughing and hollering back and forth to each other, catching up on the news. Business at Whitefield's store was booming. Colin was hard at work, filling grain and feed orders for his pa. No more games of Daniel Boone and the Indians, I thought, and it's just as well. I didn't reckon Colin would have taken kindly to my new ideas on how the game should be played.

Fiddlers and banjo players were gathering and tuning up on the porch outside the store. Usually the contest and dance were held in the barn out back of the store, it being the only place in town big enough to hold everyone. But when the store's trading began to slow down, Mr. Whitefield stepped outside and announced that the festivities would be held right out in the street in front of the store, seeing as how it was such a fine day. A cheer went up from the crowd, and people moved their wagons farther down the road to make more room.

Eli Tanner played a lick on his fiddle to get things going. Eli won the contest every year. He could play so fast and so fine that folks found themselves dancing whether they meant to or not, and they said he must have made a pact with the devil to be able to play like that. Pa said the part about the devil was nonsense, but Eli sure did have a way with a fiddle.

One by one the players took their turns. Some were good and some were pretty terrible, I reckon, but everyone got a big round of clapping from the crowd. Then Colin's twin aunts, Carolina and Georgia White-field, played a duet. It was a long hymn, very solemn and mournful, and so were their faces as they played it. Molly and I started to giggle, and Pa gave me a sharp elbow in the side. We cheered extra hard when they finally stopped.

Then Hector Whynot got up. Hector lived in a corner of the livery stable and did odd jobs to earn his keep. He'd showed up in town years back, not knowing his name or how he came to be there. Folks in town figured something had happened to his traveling party on the trip out west, and he just plain lost his memory of the whole thing. They started calling him Hector. Why not? they asked, since he doesn't know his real name. Hector Whynot he became, and it seemed to suit him fine. Whatever had happened to Hector, somewhere in his life he'd learned to play the fiddle, that was for sure. We cheered and clapped when he was through.

But Eli won the contest hands down. He played a long song, too. It started out slow and built till it was so wild and fast that folks were stomping and cheering and whistling. Then it began to wind down so sweet and sad it felt like he was running that bow over all the feelings you had inside and making them rise up in your throat at the same time. There were tears streaming down folks' faces and they didn't even know it, they were so caught up in the music. When Eli finished, there was dead quiet in the street before we recovered enough to clap and show our appreciation. Pa whistled between his teeth so loud Molly and I had to cover our ears. Mr. Whitefield made a speech and handed Eli the five-dollar gold piece that was that year's prize, and we all headed for our wagons and picnic baskets.

After supper people napped or talked quietly, enjoying the warmth of the sun and the company of other people after the loneliness and isolation of winter. I lay on my back in the wagon bed, my face turned to the sun, listening to the soft sounds of babies fussing, mothers soothing, horses whinnying, voices talking and laughing. I've got to get Pa to teach me how to whistle like that, I thought. Feeling peaceful and happy, I drifted off to sleep.

I woke to the sound of instruments being tuned, and Colin's voice in my ear. "Nathan," he said, "can you help me? Pa wants me to spread some straw on the muddy spots in the street so folks can dance."

"Sure," I answered, climbing out of the wagon bed. When we finished our task, a cheer went up from the crowd. Colin began clowning around, bowing and waving, so I did, too. Then the music started, and the street filled with people dancing. I saw Pa dancing with Molly, playing his mouth harp at the same time. I saw Miss Georgia Whitefield headed my way through the crowd, and quick ran up to stand behind Eli before she could ask me to dance. From behind Eli's flying hands, I grinned as Pa was whirled about, first by Miss Georgia, then Miss Carolina, then any number of ladies. For his part, it looked like Pa was having the time of his life.

Molly and her friends were practicing dance steps on the edges of the crowd and giggling. When she looked up to where I was standing, I did an imitation of how they looked. She stuck out her tongue at me, and we both laughed.

When the musicians took a break, Eli turned around to me. "You play the fiddle, boy?" he asked.

"No, sir," I said, "but I'd sure like to learn."

"You get yourself a fiddle and come see me," he said, and turned back to his playing.

I didn't move for the rest of the night. I just watched Eli's fingers and listened to that sweet, sweet music. I thought I'd give anything to be able to play like that. When the dance was over and the crowd began drifting away, Eli put his fiddle in its case. Seeing me still there, he said again, "You want to learn to fiddle, you come see me," and he headed off into the night.

Pa and Molly and I found each other and walked to the wagon together, Pa in the middle with an arm around each of us.

"Did you two have a good time?" he asked.

"Yes!" we both answered eagerly.

On the way home, we all sat on the front seat, cuddled under the quilts, Molly and I on either side of Pa, leaning on his shoulders. "Good," he said, "you'll hold me up. Go on, Job, take us home now, that's a good boy."

The swaying of the wagon in the soft, damp darkness, the warmth of Pa's body next to mine, and the steady *clop clop* of Job's hooves soon lulled me to sleep. When we reached the cabin, Pa sent us inside to bed while he took care of unhitching Job. As I climbed under the covers, I realized with surprise that I hadn't thought about Weasel once, all day long.

19

WE started plowing the
next day. It was hard work. My job was to follow
along behind the plow and pick up any rocks that were
turned up and carry them over to the rock pile. There
were lots of 'em. Pa said you'd think we planted rock
seeds last year the way they kept turning up. Later,
when plowing and planting were done, we'd add them
to the stone wall. We worked long days, but it was
good to be outside, and to feel the dark earth warming
in the sun, getting ready to take in our crop seeds.

We talked about the dance, recalling this or that,
enjoying it all over again in the remembering. Molly
teased Pa about dancing so much with Miss Abigail
Baldwin, and for the first time I could recall, I saw

Pa blush a deep red. He mumbled something and looked away, and I realized with a start that Pa might marry again some day. Nothing stays the same, I knew that now. I thought about Mama and how she'd most likely be glad to have someone looking after us.

I told Pa what Eli had said to me the night of the dance.

"Would you like to learn to fiddle?" he asked, looking at me curiously.

"Yes, sir," I said. "I'd like to be able to play like that, to make folks feel so—so—" I stammered, not able to put words to what I felt about Eli's playing. "So good."

Pa said he reckoned he knew what I meant. He thought just maybe, if we had a good crop this year, he could see about getting me a fiddle, and he figured that on our trips to town we could arrange to have me and Eli get together.

"And, Pa," I said, "could you teach me how to whistle the way you were doing at the dance?"

Pa showed me how to pull my lower lip back tight over my lower teeth, squish my tongue behind my back teeth, and force air out between the tip of my tongue and my two front teeth. I practiced all morning, but nothing came out but a lot of air and spit. Then, as I dropped a big rock onto the pile, a whistle came out. After a few more tries, I stood up, looked toward

Pa, and whistled to him, loud and long. Job's ears pricked up, and Pa turned around to smile and wave. We spent the rest of the day whistling back and forth, trying to outdo each other.

It was good to know Pa needed me, and putting in a good crop and maybe being able to buy a fiddle with the extra money were what I began mostly to think about. A whole month passed by before I even knew it.

One day in the middle of May, Pa and I were out in the new field, digging around the base of a stump so we could hitch Job to it and pull it out. Suddenly we heard Molly's voice, high and excited.

"Papa! Nathan! Come quick!"

We could see her standing at the stone wall, looking at something in her hands. Leaving off work on the stump, we hurried to where Molly stood, reading a letter.

She finished and looked up at us, her eyes all shiny and wet. "Read this," she said. "It's from Ezra."

Pa and I read together.

Dear Molly,
Your letter was true. I am gon to Kansis to find her kin. Tell Nathan be happy in the hat. Weezl is small now. I remmber you allwaze.

Your frend, Ezra

"And look at this. It was wrapped up in the letter." Molly held out something that dangled from a thin strip of leather. It was a locket, carved from bone and polished and oiled till it gleamed shiny white. There were two rounded halves, held together by a clasp. The face of a young girl was carved on the front half, and, crude though it was, anyone could see that it was Molly—her wide-set eyes, turned-up nose, curving smile, even her bangs and a hint of her braid.

"Open it," she said, her face beaming with pleasure.

I pulled open the clasp, and the two halves opened to reveal a lock of Ezra's dark hair.

"So I won't forget him," she said softly. "And this is for you, Nathan." She handed me a tall black hat.

I took the hat, remembering how solemn and dignified Ezra had looked in it, and how sad. Then I could see his face twisting with sudden hatred when he saw Weasel across the river. But Ezra was going to Kansas now, leaving Weasel behind.

"He'll be happy now, won't he, Papa?" asked Molly.

"It sure looks like he's going to try," Pa answered.

"What does he mean, though, 'Weasel is small now'?" she asked, looking puzzled.

Pa looked at me. "What do you think, son?"

"I think he means that—" I struggled, finding it as hard to speak my thoughts as if I was the one who had no tongue. "I think he means that now he can see so much more." I spread my arms wide to take in the forest and the sky and Kansas and the whole world beyond. "Weasel's just little compared to it all."

I stopped, feeling foolish. We all stood quiet for a minute, grinning at each other, looking at the hat and the locket and the letter and thinking of Ezra's going to Kansas to find his wife's people.

WEASEL's dead, it's true, but in some ways I don't think he'll ever die. There's those of us who'll never be the same because of knowing him. And even if Weasel's not around, there's likely to be someone else like him, or some other kind of meanness and sorrow and sadness. But there's plowing and planting, and kinfolk and Kansas, and whistling and fiddling, too. That's what Ezra wanted to tell me, I think. And I reckon if he can let go of hating Weasel, I can, too.

If I could fiddle like Eli, I could tell the story better than with words, maybe, 'cause it seems to me life's like Eli's playing. There's everything in it. Without the sad parts, the rest wouldn't sound so sweet.

It's good to have Ezra's hat, but I don't need it to remember him. I won't ever forget Ezra, or what happened to his wife and to the Shawnees. They'll be part of every song I play.